D1459275

THE FOUR-LEAVED SHAMROCK

The Four-leaved Shamrock

AND OTHER STORIES

by

Sinéad de Valera

ILLUSTRATED BY EILEEN COGHLAN

FALLONS

Also by Sinead de Valera

FAIRY TALES

THE EMERALD RING

THE STOLEN CHILD

Published by Fallons Educational Supply Company, C. J. Fallon
Limited, Kingsbridge, Dublin. Belfast: 31 King Street. London: 1
Furnival Street, Holborn. Printed by Mount Salus Press Limited in the
Republic of Ireland, Tritonville Road, Sandymount, Dublin.

CONTENTS

To my grandson, Sean O Cuiv

The Four-leaved Shamrock

(Time about a hundred years ago)

> "I'll seek a four-leav'd shamrock
>   In all the fairy dells,
> And if I find the charmed leaves
>   Oh! how I'll weave my spells."
>   — *Old song.*

"THIS is a free day from school," said Pat. "Yes," said his brother Eamonn. "I am glad the weather is so fine. We can stay out all day."

Pat, aged thirteen, and Eamonn, a year younger, were the sons of Tom O'Byrne, a small farmer in County Kildare. There was another brother, Brian, two years younger than Eamonn, along with a baby sister named Sheila.

"Do you remember the story old Dan Malone told us last night?" asked Pat.

"Yes," said Eamonn, "the one about the four-leaved shamrock. I wish I could find the shamrock for Dan said, if you had it, you could get anything you wanted."

"Now," said Pat, "when we have a free day from school we ought to go and search for it. Will you come, Brian?"

Brian thought for a moment. "I would like to go," he said, "but I want to help Mother. She is very tired because Sheila was cross last night and Mother got very little sleep."

"Much help you can be to her," said Eamonn.

"Well, I can rock the cradle and feed the chickens and bring in the turf."

7

"Oh, you are a great housekeeper," said Pat. "Come along, Eamonn. If we find the shamrock we will be sure to get rich."

"And then," said Eamonn, "we can give Mother a lot of money and that will be better for her than minding Sheila."

The two boys went off.

After a short time the mother came in from the fields where she had been milking.

"Where are Pat and Eamonn?" she asked.

"They have gone out, Mother," said Brian. "They were glad to have a free day. The weather is so fine."

"Well, Brian, they could have helped their father if they had stayed at home, but I suppose young people must have a bit of sport. What about yourself, Brian?"

"I am happy here, Mother. There is plenty I can do about the house."

When Tom O'Byrne came in for the midday meal he was disappointed that Pat and Eamonn were not at home. "Where are the boys?" he asked. "I thought they would come and help me with the work."

"They went out some time ago," said the Mother.

"Indeed, Mary, they might have stayed in to do some work. I can't afford to pay for help and it is hard to get everything done without it. There is a long winter before us and I don't know how I am to get the rent together."

"Well, Tom," said his wife, trying to speak cheerfully, "we have seen hard days before and with God's help we will be able to manage to get through all the trials as we did last winter."

When the father returned home in the evening the boys were still absent.

Now, where were they? After leaving home

They stooped down to look at the shamrock

they went along the lanes and through the fields looking for the magic shamrock. When they had walked for some time along a road they came towards a big house with a garden in front. There was a woman standing at the gate.

In this house there lived a rich man. O'Donovan was his name. He was a great scholar and spent most of his time among his books. To the people around he seemed silent and strange. They spoke of him as The Lonely Man. He was, however, very kind and generous to those in need.

Biddy Farrell, a middle-aged woman, was his sole attendant. Biddy was born in a little cottage near the big house. She had lived all her life in the neighbourhood and knew everyone for miles around. "Oh," said Eamonn, "we are in luck. There is Biddy Farrell at the gate. She knows everything about plants and herbs."

"Yes," said Pat, "and she gets a lot of knowledge from The Lonely Man."

"Well, my lads," said Biddy, when they had reached the gate. "What brings you here?"

"The school was closed and the weather was so fine we came out for the day," said Pat.

"And where is Brian, your young brother?" asked Biddy.

"He stayed at home to help in the house," said Eamonn.

"And you two left your mother to do the work and came out to enjoy yourselves. Brian is the best son of the three."

"Oh no, Biddy," said Pat. "We came out to look for the four-leaved shamrock so that we would have a wish. If we find the shamrock we can wish for money for father and mother."

Biddy smiled. "It is hard to find the four-leaved shamrock," she said.

"Could you help us to get it, Biddy?" Eamonn asked.

"Now, I won't promise anything, but there are two places where it might be found. You, Pat, climb that hill over there. When you get to the top go down the other side. There is a four-leaved shamrock growing at the bottom. You must not go round the hill, but must go up one side and down the other."

"You, Eamonn, cross the bog at the end of the road and in the field on the opposite side to the bog you will find the shamrock."

"Oh, Biddy, you are very kind and good," said Pat.

"Thank you very much," Eamonn said.

Pat hurried towards the hill. He climbed it without difficulty, but when he reached the top his foot caught in a little bush and he bumped and bumped down the other side. His head hit a stone and he lay on the ground stunned and insensible.

Eamonn ran quickly through the bog. He did not notice a big hole in front of him. In he plunged into the dark bog water. He would have been drowned only that two men who were cutting turf came to his aid.

"How will we get the lad home, Bill?" said one of the men.

"I'll manage that, Larry," Bill replied. "I have my ass and cart close by here and I can bring the poor half-drowned chap home without delay."

"But what about Pat, my brother?" asked Eamonn.

"Where is he?" said Larry.

"He climbed that hill over there but I don't know where he is now."

"I'll go round the hill and see if we can find him," said Larry.

Poor Pat was just waking from the swoon when the cart came along.

Larry met Biddy as he was taking the boys home. He told her all that had happened. Tom and his wife were so glad to have the boys home again that they could think of nothing but that they were safe and well.

After hearing how Pat and Eamonn had fared in their search, Biddy went to Mr. O'Donovan's study.

"I want to speak to you, Sir," she said.

"Yes, Biddy. What sad news have you now?" asked Mr. O'Donovan with a kindly smile.

Biddy told him about the boys' adventure and of the hard times that were threatening the O'Byrne family. "And you know, Sir," she concluded, "there is a four-leaved shamrock growing in the small field at the back of their own house and none of them know it is there." Mr. O'Donovan thought for a while.

"Have you an old purse, Biddy?" he asked.

"Yes, Sir."

"Bring it to me."

Mr. O'Donovan put a number of sovereigns into the purse.

"Now, Biddy," he said, "early tomorrow morning go to the field where the shamrock is growing. Pull some of the shamrock and place the purse underneath it. Then bring little Brian to the field and let him find the shamrock and the purse."

Next morning the family were taking their breakfast when Biddy appeared. "God save all here," she said as she went into the house.

"God save you kindly," was the reply from all.

"You did not find the four-leaved shamrock, boys. Ah! Well! the best things are often found near home. Mary, may Brian come for a little walk with me."

Mary thought this was a strange request but she knew that Biddy would bring the child safely back.

"Yes, Biddy," she said, "but don't let him delay too long. I want him to be in time for school."

"Look there," said Biddy, when she and Brian had reached the place where she had put the purse.

Brian stooped down to look at the shamrock. Clasping both it and the purse in his hand he ran towards the house, leaving Biddy to follow him.

"Now, Tom," she said, "you won't fear the hard winter. God prosper you all," were her words as she hurried away.

Mary cried with joy and poor Tom nearly cried too.

"I know, Mary," he said, "who told and who heard we had the four-leaved shamrock growing in our field."

Asailin

ONE cold winter's night, Jack Kenny, his wife and family were gathered round a blazing fire in their comfortable kitchen. Jack was glad to rest after a hard day's work on the farm. His wife was sewing while her foot rocked the cradle where Billy, the youngest child, lay.

Peter was learning his lessons for the next day while Katie tried to teach the alphabet to Annie and Nora. Suddenly a sound was heard from outside the door. A sort of cry or snort followed the sound. The father opened the door. "Oh! what strange thing is this?" he exclaimed. "Peter, get the lantern." The light of the lantern showed a thin, miserable ass lying on the ground.

"Oh!" said Peter, "that is poor old Mickey Rourke's ass. I know it by the bald spot on its head. Mickey used to say the ass got a cut on his head and the hair never grew on it again."

"I suppose," said the mother, "the poor animal got nothing to eat since Mickey died more than a week ago. Indeed sometimes it was little the old man himself had to eat."

"Father," said Katie, "what will we do with the ass?"

"I think, Katie, we can't do much for it. I would say it will hardly live till morning."

"Couldn't we lift it off the cold clay and put it in the shed?" asked Peter.

"Yes," said Katie, "and leave a bit of hay and some clean water near it."

"Have your way, children," said the father, "but I don't think the poor beast will last through the night."

Just then, a neighbour, big Jim Horan, happened to be passing by. With his help, the ass was brought into the shed. Peter ran for a vessel of water and Kate got some nice clean hay.

"Well," said the mother, "that is all we can do for poor Mickey's ass."

Next morning Peter was in a nice, sound sleep when he was awakened by these words — "Get up, Peter, and come with me to see if the ass is still alive."

"It is hard to get out of my comfortable bed, Katie, but if you go and open the door of the shed, I'll follow you."

"All right, I have the lantern, for it is still dark, and there is no one awake in the house but ourselves."

When the children went into the shed they found to their delight that the ass was still alive.

"Look," said Peter, "I think he has eaten a bit of the hay. Maybe he will get strong and we can have him for our own."

The father and mother were surprised when the children told them of their experience in the morning. Later on, the mother herself went to the shed with some oats. This the animal ate with some relish. After a few days he was able to walk about. The fact that the children had cared for him so well made them wish to keep him.

In a short time he was a fine sturdy animal. His intelligence was quickened and strengthened by the love the children had for him.

"We must give him a name," said Katie, "and let it be an Irish one."

"I remember," said Peter, "poor Mickey when driving the ass used to say, 'Now, Asailin, off we go.' Let us call him Asailin."

Asailin was now a big, handsome donkey.

"He is a fine sturdy brute," said the father, "but

we don't really want him. He is of no use on the farm."

"Oh, Jack," said the mother, "he may not be much use but the children love him and he loves them. We can't judge things for their use only. If we did what would we think of the primroses and cowslips ? "

"You are right, Mary ; the fact that he adds to the children's happiness is service in itself."

Some of the neighbours' children used to enjoy rides on Asailin. There was a boy called Bobby Martin among the group. He was not as kind as the others. He liked to tease Asailin. One day he brought him a bucket full of dirty, bad-smelling water. Of course, Asailin refused to drink. Worse than this, another day he tied an old tin can to his tail. This last act caused so much anger among his companions that he was not allowed to join in the play any more.

The children arranged to have a sports day with Asailin. Each child was to ride on him round the field without bridle or saddle. The one who did the round in the shortest time was to get the prize. Bobby asked to be allowed to join in the game.

"No," came in a chorus, "he will not be allowed."

"He was cruel to Asailin," said Peter, "and should not be let take part in the game." Bobby began to cry. Kind-hearted Katie was sorry for him.

"Let us give him a chance," she said. "I am sure he will be kind to Asailin from now on. Won't you, Bobby ? "

"Yes," said Bobby in the midst of his sobs.

The children, one by one, mounted the ass. He ran round the field with each and seemed to enjoy the sport. Bobby was the last to mount. Asailin started off but quickly went off the track to a

The little ass was lying down in the stable

corner of the field where there was a large stag-
nant pool. When he reached the pool he raised up
his hind feet, and poor Bobby found himself sitting
in the dirty water.

On Christmas morning the father asked the
children would they like to go to the stable to wish
Asailin a happy Christmas.

" Oh, yes, yes," came the answer from all. When
they reached the stable, their delight was unbounded. There was Asailin yoked to a lovely
little car.

" Oh, Mother," said Peter, " I can now drive you
into the village to get the provisions and all you
want from the shops."

Time went on and the ploughing season arrived.
The father took the two horses and went some
miles away to a friend's house to help in the work.

" I will be back the day after tomorrow," he said
as he was going off.

Night came on and all the children were in bed.
The mother had many little jobs to do. She was
just finishing up her work when she heard a
scream from the cradle. She lifted the baby. He
seemed to stiffen in her arms. His cry wakened
Katie and Peter.

" Oh, Mother," said Katie, " I think poor Billy
has convulsions. He looks like Julia Dolan's child
that died last year. I was in the house when the
doctor came. He said he could have saved the
child if he had been called in time."

" Oh, what will we do ? " said the mother.
" Your father has the horses and no one will be
able to get the doctor in time."

" Mother," said Peter, " I'll yoke Asailin and we
will reach the doctor's house in no time."

When Peter reached Dr. O'Toole's house he, by
good luck, found the doctor getting out of his car.

" Oh, Doctor," Peter said, " will you come

quickly ?　Our baby will die if you do not come at once." The good man did not hesitate.　He jumped into his own car and was soon in the house where he was to bring such relief.

"Mrs. Kenny," he said, "I am only just in time, but don't be uneasy, we will save the little fellow." Billy was his bright little self after a few days. When the father reached home he heard all that had happened.　"Now, Jack," said his wife, "you see how useful Asailin has been.　He was the means of saving Billy's life."　Asailin lived to a ripe old age and remained to the last the friend and loved companion of all the family.

The Magic Waters

SOME time after the great famine there lived in a little house near the Donegal coast a woman named Nuala. She had a hard life. Her husband had died when her only child, Donal, was very young. She worked hard but it was almost impossible to get a living from their small farm.

At seven years of age, Donal was a beautiful child and the brightest and best in the school. He was very musical, though of course he had no teacher. His great delight was to play an old fiddle that had belonged to his father.

One day he and some other boys were playing in a field. The weather was very hot and Donal felt thirsty. There was a well in a corner of the field. No one would drink the water, because it was believed to be a fairy well, but Donal did not know the fairies owned it. He ran away from his companions, made a cup of his hands and took a drink. When his friends found him, he was lying unconscious beside the well.

He was brought home and lay in a sort of sleep for some days. When he wakened he could remember nothing. He was not able to learn anything at school, and was constantly doing foolish things.

"Donal is a good boy," said Nuala to her neighbour, Mary.

"Indeed he is, Nuala."

"But," said Nuala, "he is now fourteen years of age and he hasn't a bit of sense. He does the strangest things."

"Never mind, Nuala, he has a kind heart and will be sure to have good luck. You have often told me he was very clever and sensible until he took the drink from the fairy well."

Though Mary tried to cheer her friend in her worry about Donal, she herself could not help laughing at some of his mistakes and blunders.

One day his mother told him to go to the well for a can of water. Mary was in the house as he was going off.

"Hurry now," she said, "and be back here while the cat is licking her ear."

This saying among the old people meant "hurry and do the deed quickly."

Donal found the cat which was a great pet of his. He took it in his arms and brought it to the well. The two women waited a long time for his return.

"What can be keeping him?" said Nuala.

"Oh! here he is at last," said Mary as Donal approached with the can in one hand and the cat held under his coat with the other.

"Mother," he said, "I waited and waited but Puisin (the cat) wouldn't lick her ear at all."

"My poor boy, Mary," said Nuala, "will he ever get sense?"

"I tell you, Nuala," was her friend's reply, "Donal is so good and kind he will some day bring you great good luck."

Nuala struggled on trying to provide for herself and her poor foolish son. She reared poultry and got some profit from the eggs.

One day she arranged a nest and put a goose sitting on a set of eggs. Next day when she was going out to milk the goat she said to Donal, "Now, like a good boy be careful that the eggs are kept warm. Don't let the goose get off them. If you do we will have no young ones."

"All right, Mother, you may be sure I'll keep the eggs warm."

It was a very cold day. To keep the kitchen

warm Donal locked the door. He then got a handful of oats and went towards the goose.

" Well, goosie, would you like a grain of oats ? " he said.

In his awkward way he let some fall before he reached the nest. The goose rose from the nest. Donal in fright tried to force her back. She pecked him and hurt him badly. Then she flew up on the table.

" Oh ! Oh ! Oh ! what will I do ? " thought poor Donal. " The eggs will get cold if the goose does not sit on them. I'll make a goose of myself I'll sit on them and keep them warm."

His mother returned and found the door barred.

" Let me in, Donal," she cried.

" Mother, I'm a goose," came the reply.

" Let me in, let me in," said the mother.

" I can't let you in. The eggs will get cold if I leave them."

" Oh ! what will I do ? " said the poor distracted mother to Cormac, a boy who was passing.

" Wait, ma'am," said he, " I'll get in through the window."

When Cormac opened the door Nuala found Donal still trying to keep the eggs warm. She pulled him off the nest and found the eggs broken.

The poor woman began to cry.

" Don't cry, ma'am," said Cormac.

" The woman in the big house asked my mother yesterday where could she get a hatching goose. She said she had some very special eggs and she wanted a good goose to bring out the goslings. She would give any price to get a suitable bird."

" My goose is a great mother," said Nuala. " She brought out a fine set of young ones last year."

" Well," said Cormac, " if you tie her legs together I will take her up to the big house and bring you back the money."

Cormac was not long in returning. The sum he got was more than Nuala would have got for the goslings.

One day Nuala had a bad cold and had to stay in bed. Mary came in to tell her of two events which had taken place in the village that morning.

"I have bad and good news," she said. Poor Tom the tailor died this morning and in the next house there was a wedding. Maurice Gallagher and Betty Carroll were married."

"Oh!" said Nuala, "they will think I am a very bad neighbour not to have gone to either of the houses."

"I went to both this morning," said Mary, "but I can't go again for I left the baby in the cradle with no one to mind him but his little sister, Eileen, so I must hurry home. I'll tell you what I'll do. I'll write too little notes and send them with Donal to both houses."

"It is well for you, Mary," said Nuala. "You can read and write. I can't do either and though Donal went to school he knows nothing. I will be very thankful if you will send a note to each house."

"Now, Donal," said Mary as she gave him one of the notes, "be careful to keep this in your right hand and leave it at the corpse house. Keep the other in your left hand and leave it in the house where the bride and bridegroom are."

"All right, ma'am," said Donal and off he went.

As he was nearing the village he tumbled over a large stone. The notes fell from his hands. He picked them up and mixed them up. The newly married pair were greatly astonished to read: "I am very sorry for your trouble. Deepest sympathy." The poor widow got the other message: "Congratulations. Long life and happiness."

Nuala was in despair when she heard how things had turned out, but everything was explained to the widow and to the bride and bridegroom.

One dark winter night Nuala was sitting at the fire knitting. Donal sat beside her with the cat in his arms. The day had been very wet but the rain had stopped as evening came on.

A gentle knock came to the door. Donal opened it. Outside stood a little woman covered in a hooded cloak.

"I am a travelling woman," she said, "looking for a night's shelter."

"Come in," said Donal, "and warm yourself at the fire."

"You are welcome to stay," said Nuala, "you can have my bed."

"No, mother, let her have my bed. Puisin and I can sleep before the fire."

"No, Donal, you know you cannot do without sleep. You must go to bed after we have had something to eat."

The strange woman remained silent.

"Donal, get the milk and bread," said Nuala.

Now, Nuala was very poor and Donal, slow and dull though he was, knew there would not be enough bread and milk for all three. He placed the food on the table and then said:

"Mother, I don't want any supper. I'll go to bed now."

"Wait," said the stranger as she took out a bag which she had kept under her cloak. From the bag she took bread, butter and a large bottle of milk.

"Oh! Mother," said Donal, "we will have a grand supper. Look at the butter."

All three enjoyed the meal and then Donal went off to bed.

The two women remained sitting at the fire.

"You son is a good boy," said the stranger. "He was willing give me his bed and to do without his supper so that I might have mine."

He gave a handful of oats to the goose

" He is the best and kindest boy in the world, but he hasn't one bit of sense. He does all sorts of queer things."

" Was he always like that ? " asked the woman.

" No, indeed. Up to the time he was seven years old he was the brightest boy in the school, but now he can't learn anything. The only thing he can do is play that old fiddle that is hanging up there. He brought it to school one day and when the master went out of the room he had all the lads dancing."

" You say he was not always as he is now. What made the change in him ? "

Brigid looked frightened. She lowered her voice. " I am nearly afraid to tell you for fear worse might happen to him."

" Have the fairies anything to do with the matter ? " asked the woman. " If they have you need not be afraid to tell me. I am proof against all charms and spells."

Nuala told the woman all about the day on which Donal was brought home from the field. She listened with great attention.

" I understand," she said, " he drank water from the well of forgetfulness." She remained silent for a moment. Then she said :

" What was caused by magic water can be cured by magic water."

" But where is the magic water to be found ? " asked Brigid.

" Will you allow your son to come with me ? We could leave the house before daybreak and return to-morrow night. I may be able to bring good luck to him."

" Yes, I will let him go with you. My neighbour Mary always said Donal would have good luck some day, because he was so good and kind."

Next morning Donal was awakened very early. He and the strange woman left the house before daybreak. They travelled a long way. As dawn appeared they reached a lane which led to the sea. They came to a cave. "We will stay here for a while," said the woman.

It was cold and hard on the rocks, but Donal was glad to rest.

The woman took from her bag some bread and butter and rosy apples. When they had eaten she took Donal by the hand and led him to the outside of the cave. There was a hollow in the rocks on the top of the cave. In wet weather this hollow was filled with water which flowed down the side and formed a small waterfall.

The woman took from her bag a large shell. " Now," she said to Donal, " fill this shell with water from the fall, and drink the water."

Donal was thirsty and was glad to do as she asked.

As he drank, the woman chanted these words:
" 'Water from the magic fall
    Clear mist and clouds and darkness all."

For a short time after drinking, Donal felt faint and dizzy.

Then he said: " I feel as if some weight has been lifted from my brain. Everything is bright and clear to me. Let me go home to my mother at once."

It was evening when they reached home.

As Donal entered the house he took his mother in his arms and said: " Mother, here is your son home to you. Where have I been all these years ? "

" Oh ! " said the mother, " what wonderful thing has happened ? Here I have the handsome, clever boy that I knew when he was a young child."

Turning to the woman she said: " How can I thank you ? "

" I need no thanks," was the reply. " You and your son gave me a kindly welcome. If you had

turned me from your door I would not have used
my power to help."

"Won't you tell us your name?" said Donal.

"Coonav is my name and my work is to help
good and kind people. I never use my power for
those who are hard and selfish. I must leave you
now. *Slan agaibh* (good-bye)."

She opened the door and passed quickly into the
darkness of the night.

From that time onwards Donal was sensible and
intelligent. The kind schoolmaster gave him
lessons. He learned quickly. Bill, the blacksmith,
who was growing old was glad to take him into
the forge.

When Bill died Donal kept on the work. After
some time he and his mother were comfortable
and happy.

Donal was loved by all the people around. He
was constantly asked to play his fiddle at the
dances, and he brought joy and mirth wherever
he went.

The Land of Tantalizers

ONCE upon a time there lived in a little house among the Dublin hills a woman named Una. Her husband had died when her two children, Sean and Brigid, were very young.

Sean was a strange boy. He gave a lot of trouble to his mother and sister. He was for ever teasing and annoying them. Even the animals did not escape from what he considered his jokes and tricks.

" Sean," the mother would say, " stop pulling the cat's whiskers." But when he ceased annoying the cat he began pulling the dog's tail.

Brigid had a pet hen called Chucky. It was a delight to the little girl to go to the hen house to find an egg.

One day she found the poor bird lying on the ground. Her legs were tied together. Beside her was a cracked egg.

Sean came to the door. " Chucky, Chucky, Chucky," said he.

Quick as a flash, Brigid threw the egg with steady aim. It hit Sean straight on the nose. The laugh was now on Brigid's side as she saw him trying to clear the egg from his face and clothes.

One night the mother went out to get some turf. Brigid was very tired.

" I am very sleepy," she said. " Now, Sean, don't make noise. I am going to bed."

No sooner was his sister in bed than Sean began to shout at the top of his voice.

" Close your eyes and go to sleep, Brigid," he said, as he rattled a poker and tongs and made all the noise he could.

29

Shortly after the mother returned, a knock came to the door.

" Come in," said Una, the mother.

" Stay out," said Sean, as he stood with his back against the door.

The mother pulled him away and in came a strange-looking old man. He had a long white beard and wore a hat with a pointed crown. His cloak was so long that it almost covered his feet.

" You are welcome," said Una as she placed a stool near the fire.

Sean was about to pull the stool away but the old man was too quick for him. He turned and glared at him with a look that warned Sean that he had better not try that trick.

" It is a very cold night," said he. " I am glad to warm myself at this nice fire."

" Indeed you are welcome," said Una as she put some milk in a saucepan which she placed on the fire.

" Take this," she said, handing a cup of the hot milk to the stranger.

" I am very thankful for your kindly welcome," said he.

Sean pushed the man's arm intending to spill the milk but the cup was held in a firm grasp.

With a knowing look the man turned the cup so as to let some of the hot milk fall on Sean's bare foot.

" Oh ! I'm scalded," Sean yelled.

The stranger smiled and said :—

" If a joke you cannot take, then a joke you should not make."

He then took a phial from under his cloak and poured from it something which cured the pain at once.

The old man was really one of the fairy people. He had great magic powers.

In came a strange-looking old man

" Mother," called Brigid from the bedroom, " was Sean badly hurt ? " For though he teased her so much, she was very fond of him.

The mother went into the room to tell Brigid everything was well. When she returned to the kitchen there was no one there. Both Sean and the stranger had disappeared.

She opened the door and looked out. Not a sound was to be heard.

She ran along the road for some distance. All was dark and silent.

" Oh," she thought, " that was a fairy man. He has taken poor Sean to the fairy fort. I will never see him again."

She went back into the house.

After a short time Cait, a neighbour woman, came in.

" What is the matter ? " she asked when she saw Una sitting at the fire crying.

" Oh! Cait, my poor son has been taken away by a fairy man."

" I am sorry for you, Una, but the fairies do not always keep the people they take with them. Maybe it was a good fairy that took Sean and for some good reason, too. If that is so you will surely have him back before long. What was the fairy like ? "

" He seemed to be good and kind," said Una.

" Well, I tell you Sean will be back by twelve o'clock to-night, but I warn you not to ask him where he has been. The fairies put a spell of silence and secrecy on those who have been with them."

" Then you think the fairies won't harm him.

" No, they won't harm him. That old man took him for some good purpose. Leave the door on the latch. I'm sure he will return at midnight."

" I hope your words will come true, Cait. Could

you stay with me till twelve o'clock ? "

" Yes, I can and will be glad to stay."

The fairy took Sean outside the door before the boy had realized he was leaving the house.

There standing on the road was a white horse. The man whisked Sean on to its back. He himself jumped up in front of him. Like a flash, the horse rushed off.

After a short time they reached a valley in the midst of the hills. The fairy man alighted. He lifted Sean from the horse. The horse vanished.

" Remain here till I come for you," said the fairy.

The cold air had made Sean very hungry. To his delight, he saw a tree laden with fine, rosy apples. He turned towards the tree. Just as he was about to pick a big apple he heard a voice shout " Stop ! " An ugly old hag came out from behind the tree. She had a black stick in her hand. With this she touched the tree. Immediately the apples turnd to sand which fell to the ground. The hag vanished.

As Sean looked round he saw a fountain from which flowed clear, sparkling water.

There was a stone cup near it.

" Well," thought he, " if I cannot eat, I can at least have a drink."

He stooped down to take the cup. Again he heard the word " Stop " as the hag re-appeared. She struck the fountain. The water turned into grit and pebbles. Again she vanished.

Poor Sean was now very tired.

His strength seemed gone. " Oh ! if only I could rest and sleep," he thought.

All at once he saw a bed of beautiful soft moss and a little mound like a pillow at one end. He was about to lie down and rest when again he heard the word " Stop ". The hag appeared and struck the moss. It turned into hard rock.

As the hag vanished he saw the fairy man coming towards him.

" Oh! where am I ? " asked Sean.

" You are in the land of Tantalizers," said the man.

" Why did you bring me here ? "

" To show you how cruel and wrong it is to tease and torment people as you do."

" Let me go, please, and I will never tease or torment anyone again."

" You will return for the sake of your good, kind mother."

" Yes, she will be wondering where I have been."

" Now when you return you must not tell anyone, even your mother, that you were in the Land of Tantalizers. If you do I will put a spell on you and bring you back here again."

The fairy blew a little whistle. Immediately the white horse appeared.

When Sean reached his home the horse was quickly lost to sight.

At twelve o'clock while Una and Cait were still sitting at the fire they heard the door opening. Cait put her finger on her lips.

Sean came in. He said good-night to them and went to his room.

When the mother and Brigid came into the kitchen in the morning they were surprised to see everything ready for breakfast. It was Sean who had got up early and had done the work.

From that time onwards he was a joy in the home. Everyone noticed the change in his conduct and character.

" I believe," said the mother to her friend, Cait, " it was the fairy man that brought me the good luck."

" You may be sure of it, Una," said Cait. " Your kindly welcome to the stranger brought you a rich reward."

The Mountain Wolf

L ONG, long ago there lived among the
mountains of Kerry a rich man named
Brendan and his wife Cliona. They had three
children, twin boys Ruairi and Fergus aged twelve
years and Brian aged ten.

One day in early autumn the children were in
the garden with Sheila, their nurse. Sheila had
been nurse to their mother.

The boys loved her and she loved them. Brian
was her special favourite, because he was particularly gentle and kind to her.

"Tell us a story, please, Sheila," said Ruairi.

"I think, boys, by this time you have heard all
my stories."

"But we like to hear them over again," said
Fergus.

"Well, what one will I tell you ? "

The boys thought for a while. Then Brian said :
" Tell the one about the wolf."

" Indeed I thought you were all tired of that but
if you wish me to tell it, here it is :

" You have heard of the poor, lonely widow who
lives in the little house beside the mill."

" Yes," came the chorus.

" Well, there is a sad story about her only child,
Fiachra.

" One evening as darkness was coming on
Fiachra was standing at the door of his house. An
old hag came along. She was so strange looking,
that Fiachra thought she could not belong to this
world. Her black eyes glared at him. She drew
back her large cloak and from under it a fierce wolf
appeared. It snarled and growled. Fiachra was

35

afraid it was about to attack him. He hit it with a stick which he had in his hand.

"The woman held back the wolf but turned to Fiachra and said: 'Before the night falls you yourself will have the shape of the animal you would have hurt. You will never recover your own form, unless someone calls you by your name, Fiachra.'

"A mist came over the boy's eyes. When it cleared both the hag and wolf had disappeared.

"The spell, however, fell on poor Fiachra. When his mother came to the door to bring him in, he was not there. All she could see in the gathering darkness was a wolf hurrying towards the forest.

"The only one who saw what had happened was an old crippled man who sat near the house. He could not rise from his chair to call for help. It was from him I heard the story."

"Where is he now ? " asked Fergus.

"The old man died some months ago."

"Poor Fiachra!" said Brian.

"Yes, poor lad, he has never been seen since, and all the wolves have gone from the forest, except one, which seems to have escaped from the hunters."

"And the mother never found her son," said Fergus.

"No, never, and she is a very sad old woman living all alone."

Just then a messenger came to say that the boys were to go to their mother. She wanted them to go with her to the heather field.

Mother and children walked about the field for some time.

"Oh! look, Mother," said Fergus. "I have found a piece of white heather. That will bring me good luck."

The mother laughed. "Indeed, my boy, many

people believe white heather brings good luck, but, white or purple, it is pleasant to see the heather bells stretching out over the field."

Just then the mother uttered a sharp cry:

" Boys, there is a wasp's nest. Run from the field at once."

The boys hurried out. The mother was the last to leave the field. A crowd of the wasps settled on her dress. When she reached home it was found she had been severely stung.

Th doctor was sent for, but, by the time he arrived the poison had gone through her system. All kinds of remedies were tried, but the stings were so great and so numerous that poor Cliona lost the use of her limbs and it seemed as if she would never be able to walk again.

One day, about a year after the sad happening, the family were chatting together after lunch. Felim, a man from the garden, came to tell them that Conn, the travelling man, had come to the house.

" Make him welcome," said the father, " the children love to hear his songs and stories."

" May we go to him at once, Father ? " asked Ruairi.

" Yes, of course. He will be as glad to see all of you as you will be to see him. I myself will come down later on. I wish your mother could come, too."

" Don't trouble about me," said the mother. " I am happy when all of you are enjoying yourselves."

When the boys went into the kitchen they found Conn sitting at the table having a good meal. It was a pleasant meeting.

" Welcome, Conn," was the greeting from all three. " It is more than a year since you were here before."

" You must have a lot to tell," said Ruairi.

" Well, I have some news but, before I begin to talk, tell me about your parents."

" Father will soon be here to see you, but poor mother cannot come," said Fergus.

" I hope she is not ill," said Conn.

The boys then told him all about the visit to the heather field and its sad result.

When the father came in, the old man almost cried as he said: " I am broken hearted to hear that the kind mother has had such ill luck."

" I know how sorry you are, Conn. The home is not the same happy place since she became ill."

" Can no cure be found for her ? " Conn asked.

" No. We have had the cleverest doctors that can be found, but no one can cure her."

The old man was silent for a moment. Then he said :—

" Wasp stings sometimes resist all human skill but I would not despair. There is a rare bush that grows on the side of a mountain near the forest. It has large purple berries. The juice from these berries, when heated over a turf fire, is said to have wonderful healing power."

" Could we possibly get these berries ? " asked the father.

" Yes, but they must be collected by a relative of the patient."

" Unfortunately," said the father, " I must leave home to-night and I will be absent for a couple of days, but I will try to get the berries immediately after I return."

" Gathering the berries is not such an easy matter," said Conn. " There used be many wolves in the forest."

" Yes," said Ruairi, " but I heard they are all gone except one."

" That is true, my boy," said Conn, " but that

one is very watchful, and it would be dangerous for anyone to go near him."

"Well, Conn, we will see what can be done when I return," said the father. "Enjoy yourselves now, boys, while you have your friends with you."

The boys spent a very happy evening with Conn. He sang songs, played games with them, and told them stories.

From birth the twins had always slept in the one room. Their beds, presses and everything were of the same pattern.

After saying goodnight to Conn they went to their room and settled down for a talk.

"I think, Fergus," said Ruairi, "that you and I should go to the mountain and try to get the berries that would cure Mother."

"But what about the wolf?" asked Fergus.

"I have thought of that, but perhaps we could avoid him if we slipped out after dark."

"How could we find the berries in the dark?"

"We could take a lantern with us."

"Indeed, Ruairi, I would do anything to cure poor Mother."

"Well, we will steal out to-morrow night."

"All right, Ruairi. I won't be a bit afraid and I know you are as brave as a lion. We won't tell anyone we are going. I am sure we will be able to get the berries."

Next morning Ruairi told Fergus that he was sure they would succeed in their attempt to get the berries.

"I was dreaming all night that I had killed the wolf," he said.

"We had better bring hatchets with us," said Fergus.

That night the two boys left the house while everyone thought they were in bed.

They went quickly to the mountain. "Let us go round to the side where the berries are," said Ruairi.

With the hatchets held firmly on their shoulders, they marched bravely on. Just as they reached the bush they heard a snarl and, on looking towards the forest, they saw the wolf glaring at them.

At the sight, terror seized them. They dropped their hatchets and ran for their lives.

They had not been missed, but the next morning there was great wonder among the workmen at the disappearance of the hatchets.

They told Brian of their adventure but warned him to keep it a secret.

Later in the day Brian was talking to Sheila.

"Conn has told us," he said, "that there are berries growing on the mountain that would cure Mother. All the wolves are gone from the forest except one. I wonder, Sheila, would that one be Fiachra."

"Well, alanna," said Sheila, "if there was someone brave enough to go to the mountain and call out the name Fiachra, we would know if the boy is there in the form of a wolf."

Brian thought things over. He determined to go to the mountain and call out the name.

That night Brian, instead of going to his room, slipped out quietly. He took the lantern with him.

When he reached the mountain he heard a snarl and saw the wolf coming out of the forest. He was terrified. His instinct was to run, but instead he called out the name, Fiachra.

Then in fear and terror he fell to the ground in a faint.

When he regained consciousness he saw a kindly face bending over him.

Two gentle arms helped to lift him to his feet.

"Oh! Who are you?" asked Brian.

a snarling wolf came out of the forest

" I am Fiachra," was the reply.

" You have been under a cruel spell."

" And you have broken the spell. When you called the name Fiachra, the form and nature of the wolf disappeared, and I can now go home to my poor mother."

" You will have a happy meeting."

" Yes, and I may thank you for our happiness. But why did you come here ? "

" I was told there were berries on a bush which grows on the side of the mountain. These berries are said to be a cure for wasp stings. Do you know where the bush is ? "

" We will walk round the mountain and look," said Fiachra.

When the boys found the bush, Brian wondered how he could bring the berries home.

He had forgotten to bring something in which to hold them.

" I have an idea," said Fiachra. " There is a tree in the forest that has enormous broad leaves. You can carry the berries on them."

" While you, Fiachra, are getting the leaves I will begin to gather the berries. They must be gathered by someone who is related to the sufferer."

With happy hearts the boys set out for home.

When they reached Brian's house they parted, promising to meet again to talk over their wonderful adventure.

It was late when Fiachra reached his home. His mother was sleeping near a window which looked out on the street.

Fiachra tapped at the window and said softly, " Mother."

The mother turned in her sleep but did not waken.

Again Fiachra knocked and called.

This time the mother sat up in bed.

" That was a strange dream," she thought. " I was sure I heard Fiachra's voice."

Again Fiachra knocked and called.

This time the mother pulled back the curtain. Then she gave a cry and almost fainted.

" Mother," cried Fiachra, " open the door. Your own boy is home to you again."

It would be difficult to describe the delight of the pair.

Fiachra was from that day the joy of his mother's heart and her strength and comfort in her old age.

In the meantime Brian knew that there would be someone in the kitchen till a late hour.

He left the berries outside the door and went in. He found Conn and Sheila sitting at the fire having a great chat.

" Oh! avick, I thought you were in bed hours ago."

" Hush, Sheila. I have something to show to you and Conn."

He brought in the berries.

" These are the berries from the bush on the mountain," said Conn.

" Yes, Conn."

" How did you manage to get them ? "

" I will tell you later on, Conn, but will you show me how they are to be used to cure Mother ? "

Conn turned to Sheila and said :—

" Get a three-legged pot, a little water from the well outside under the ash tree, and stew the berries over a turf fire."

After some time, Conn said :—

" Now put the juice into a basin and go and bathe the patient's feet."

" Hurry, hurry, Sheila," said Brian. " We three

will now go to Mother's room."

Sheila was the first to enter the room. The mother was sitting at the fire, reading.

"Now, achushla," said Sheila, "it is time for you to be resting. I will bathe your feet and then you can go to bed."

When Cliona put her feet into the basin she uttered a cry——

"Oh! what kind of water is this?" she said. "My feet feel as they did before they lost their power."

To her great joy she soon found she could walk again.

"What wonderful thing has brought about this cure?"

"Your son Brian may be thanked for it all. It was he who went to the forest and collected the berries which were the magic cure," said Sheila proudly.

"But, Mother," said Brian, "it was Conn who told us about the berries."

"That is true," said Sheila, "but you must tell your mother how brave you were going to the mountain to face the fierce wolf."

"But, Mother, Ruairi and Fergus went to the mountain, too, but they did not know what Sheila had told me."

Sheila then gave an account of poor Fiachra's transformation.

"Well," said Cliona, "there are two very happy mothers to-night, myself and Fiachra's.

"Our suffering is now turned into great happiness. Indeed it was by the helpful knowledge and advice of Sheila and Conn that everything has come right."

All From The Sea

KING ANNLA and Queen Nessa had been married some years and had no children. This was a source of disappointment to the King. He wished to have an heir to inherit his rich dominions.

One day as he walked along the seashore, Duald, a wise druid, came towards him.

"Tell me, Duald," said the King, "will I ever have an heir to my throne?"

"Oh, King, give me a little time and I will answer that question."

Duald went into the palace grounds and cut four rods of yew. On these he wrote ogham signs.

He returned to Annla and said: "Oh, King, you will have a son but at first sight he will not be pleasing to you."

"Tell me more," demanded Annla.

"More than this has not yet been revealed to me," said Duald.

Some time after this a son was born. The Queen was very happy but she wondered why the attendants did not allow her to see the child.

"Mor," she said to her favourite waiting maid, "bring the baby to me."

Mor approached with the child but kept her hand on its forehead.

The Queen pushed the hand aside and there to her dismay she saw a dark mark above the eyebrows.

"Oh! Mor," she cried, "my poor son! The law in Eirinn is that no one with such a blemish can ever be king."

Just then Annla came into the room. When he

saw the disfigurement on the child's face, his disappointment was terrible.

"Let the child be banished!" he exclaimed as he rushed from the room.

He mounted his horse and rode away from the palace to be alone with his gloomy thoughts.

The poor Queen was in despair. Suddenly Mor sprang to her feet. "Wait, O Queen. All is not lost."

"Go," she said to one of the attendants, "and ask Duald to come here."

"What can Duald do?" asked the poor Queen.

"What *cannot* Duald do?" Mor replied.

When Duald appeared and saw the grief of the Queen, he said kindly: "Have hope. There is a way to cure this infirmity. Give me the child and let me take him with me."

"Oh!" said the Queen, "do not take him away from me."

"Give him into my keeping. I will soon return with him. It is with great joy you will see him again."

Having said these words, Duald took the child and departed.

"Do not be uneasy, O Queen," said Mor. "The wise and faithful druid will bring the child safely back."

Duald went to the seashore. He stooped down at the edge of the water and let a wave touch the forehead of the child.

"One," he counted.

He stooped again till another wave had touched the child.

"Two," he counted.

This he continued till nine waves were counted. and the blemish disappeared.

The Queen rejoiced when she saw her son free from taint or blemish.

" Oh ! " exclaimed Mor, " how has this happened ? "

" That is my secret," said Duald, " a secret which cannot be told to anyone."

" How beautiful the child is," said Mor.

After some time the King returned. He went to the Queen's room. As he approached he heard the cry of the infant. Opening the door, he called out in anger——

" Have my orders been disobeyed ? "

Mor, with a triumphant and somewhat defiant note in her voice, said——

" Here, O King, is your child. He has inherited his mother's beauty."

Annla looked in amazement at his lovely son.

" How has this wonderful change c o m e about ? " he asked.

" I do not know," said the Queen truthfully, " but now you have a son you can love and in whom you can take pride as your heir."

" You, Nessa, would have loved him even if he had remained as he was at first," said Annla, ashamed.

" Yes," said the Queen, " but I am glad that he will be a joy to your heart as well as to mine."

" But," asked the King again, " what has caused this extraordinary change ? "

" That, O King," said Duald, " is a secret which cannot be disclosed even to the parents."

" This is all very strange," replied Annla, " but I shall atone for my recent harsh behaviour by refraining from asking any more questions."

" It was through Duald's power that the blemish was removed," said the Queen. " He has the right to claim secrecy if he does not wish to tell how the change came about."

" I claim a further privilege," said Duald, " that I may choose the name by which the child will be called."

" We owe so much to your power and help,"
said the Queen, " you should if you wish have the
choice of the name."

" Let him be named Aigean " (pronounced
Agane), said Duald.

" Does not Aigean mean ocean ? " asked the
King.

" Yes," answered Duald, " the child will love the
sea and will derive much happiness from it."

" I am not surprised to hear that," said Annla.
" His mother loves the sea. I believe her pet name
as a child was *An Muruach Bheag,* that is The Little
Mermaid."

" Let us be happy in the possession of such a
beautiful child," said the Queen.

Duald's prophecy came true. Even as a little
child Aigean longed to be near the sea.

Mor, who loved him as she loved his mother,
took him to walk among the flowers in the gardens
of the palace. She brought him to the lakeside
where the wild fowl dived and swam. She showed
him the changing colours of the trees in the woods.

None of that could satisfy the child. His constant request was " Come to the sea."

He could swim when he was five years old.
Even in cold weather he liked to wade and play at
the edge of the tide.

" Don't you hear the waves talking to me,
Mor ? " he would say.

" No, asthore, I don't hear any voices."

" Oh! I hear them. When the wind is strong
they are harsh and loud. On calm days the voices
are as soft as the cooing of the doves in the woods."

Some miles away from Aigean's home was a
great castle. It stood on high ground overlooking
the sea. Diarmuid, a great chief, lived there with
his wife Ina and their daughter Alainn (the
beautiful).

At the mouth of the cave was an ugly old hag

Diarmuid and King Annla were great friends. Alainn, who was some years younger than Aigean, often visited the palace with her parents. The wish of the parents on both sides was that the friendship between the young pair would end in marriage.

After some years, Ina became very ill.

"I fear, Diarmuid," she said, "I shall never recover."

"Oh! don't think of anything like that," said Diarmuid. "What would Alainn and I do without you?"

"Well, if I do not get better will you send for my sister's daughter?"

"I do not believe you are going to die, but to please you I will send for your niece, Finola."

"Yes, do. She is about Alainn's age, and as both her parents are dead she will be glad to have a home here. She will be a friend and companion for Alainn."

In a short time Ina was dead. Shortly before her death Finola arrived at the castle. She did not resemble her cousin in appearance. She had good features but her hard, cold nature was reflected in her face.

Diarmuid grieved much for the loss of his wife. He hoped that the companionship of Finola would lighten Alainn's grief and loneliness.

As time went on, Alainn began to see that she could never win the affection or even the friendship of her cousin. Finola watched with jealous eyes the attention shown to Alainn by all who came to the castle.

One day she came into the garden where Alainn was gathering flowers.

"How is it, Alainn," she said, "that no one seems to notice me when you are present?"

"Oh! Finola, that is mere fancy on your part."

" Indeed it is not fancy. The fact is you wish to keep me in the background."

" How can you say that ? Have you not dresses and jewels as beautiful as I have ? "

" Which of my jewels could compare with your pearl necklace ? "

" That necklace, Finola, belonged to my mother. She asked me to promise that I would never part with it. It is said to have been made by the fairies and that it has the power to protect the wearer from the power of charms or spells."

" Good fortune seems to come to you from all directions. Everyone praises your singing. No one will ever think of me while you are near."

Envy and jealousy of her cousin grew stronger and stronger in Finola's mind. She came to hate Alainn and wished she could find means to banish her from the castle.

As the great festival of Bealtaine (May 1st) approached, Diarmuid decided to give a ball.

" Now, girls," he said to Alainn and Finola, " wear your most beautiful dresses and jewels."

Aigean was among the guests. Alainn and Finola were standing together when he arrived. They both welcomed him and then Alainn turned to greet some other friends.

" Don't you think Alainn's name was well chosen ? " said Aigean to Finola. " She is very beautiful."

He did not see the frown on Finola's face as she turned away.

Still greater was Aigean's admiration for Alainn when he listened to her beautiful singing. Her song, ' The Sad Sea Maiden ', especially charmed him.

When the guests had departed Finola went to walk alone by the sea. She was troubled with bitter and jealous thoughts as she reached the cliffs at the far end of the strand.

At the foot of the cliffs was a great cave.

Suddenly a voice came from out the cave: "Who comes near my home in the light of the early dawn. ?"

Finola stood still. At the mouth of the cave appeared a hideously ugly old hag.

"Oh!" thought Finola, "the Cave Witch."

"Forgive me," she said, "I did not mean to disturb you. I am a very unhappy girl."

"Sit down on these rocks and tell me the cause of your unhappiness. Perhaps I can help you, but I must get a reward if I do."

"You know the castle at the far end of the strand," said Finola.

"I know the castle and I know ever person and place for miles round."

"You know me, then, and you know my cousin, Alainn."

"I know you all."

"Now Alainn is very beautiful and everyone loves her."

"I know that."

"Prince Aigean loves her."

"Yes."

"No one will ever love me while she is there to charm all who meet her."

The witch chuckled. "You would like to have her out of the way?" she said.

"Yes. No one will ever care for me while she is present."

"Well," said the witch, "I hate her father because he would never let me near the castle. He is afraid of the power of my charms and spells. I will now give him reason to fear them more. I will put his beautiful daughter under a spell."

"You cannot do that. She has a pearl necklace which is proof against all spells."

" Get me that necklace as a reward for my help and Alainn will never trouble you again."

" But how shall I procure the necklace ? Alainn wears it constantly."

" Alainn is always anxious to please you."

" Yes, she tries to win the affection which I can never give her."

" Early to-morrow afternoon ask her to go with you for a sail in your boat. You are very clever with the oars. When you are a good distance from the land, ask her to take the oars for a while. Then snatch the necklace from her."

" But she will resist."

The witch drew a pin from her cloak.

" Have patience," she said," " till I tell you all. While Alainn is struggling to regain the necklace pierce her arm with this pin. She will be changed immediately into a beautiful white sea bird and will retain nothing of her human nature except a sweet singing voice."

" Will she ever regain her own form ? "

" Not unless a human being sets foot on the island where she has her nest."

" Where is the island ? " asked Finola.

" It is far away on the ocean and no one has ever yet landed on it. Go back now. It is already time for me to rest. Be sure to bring me the necklace."

Finola returned to the castle with a firm determination to keep the necklace for herself. She knew the witch could not harm her while she had it in her possession.

Next day she went to Alainn's room.

" It is a lovely day, Alainn," she said. " I am going to take the boat and go for a row. Will you come with me ? "

" You know how much I love the sea, Finola, and you are very clever with the oars. Of course I'll come. Wait till I put on my necklace. It will save me from all harm," she added laughingly.

Ronan, an old sailor, brought out the boat.

" The day has been beautiful so far," he said, " but I do not like the look of these clouds over there. I would not advise a long sail fearing a sudden squall should come on."

" Oh, Ronan," said Alainn, " you don't know what a clever oarswoman my cousin is. We shall be quite safe."

The boat was a long way out to sea when Finola said : " Alainn, my arms are tired. Will you take the oars for a while ? "

Alainn had rowed for some time when Finola sprang forward and snatched the necklace.

Alainn was so much astonished that for a moment she remained still. In that moment Finola pierced her arm with the witch's pin. Immediately she was changed into a beautiful white bird. The bird rose into the air.

Finola fastened the necklace to the bottom of the boat. She dare not be seen wearing it, as she returned to the castle.

When she was still some distance from the shore a sudden squall came on. It was almost impossible to keep the boat moving in the face of the wind. She dropped one of the oars. The boat made a sudden lurch and she was thrown into the swirling water.

Diarmuid and all the household were on the shore anxiously awaiting the return of the boat. Darkness came on and with it despair in all their hearts.

Next morning at daybreak Ronan went down to the strand. He saw a boat drifting on the sea some distance from the land.

He went in another boat to tow it in. When it landed the necklace was found twisted in the boards at the bottom.

Diarmuid himself came down to the strand.

"Both girls are gone," said he. "The necklace must have fallen from Alainn's neck. No harm could have come to her while she wore it. I wish I knew her fate and that of Finola, too."

Knowledge of Finola's fate was not long delayed. Her body was washed ashore next morning.

Diarmuid was now a sad and lonely man. His friends from far and near came to try to console him. Among them were Aigean and his parents.

"You, Aigean," said Diarmuid, "are a child of the sea. I only wish you could bring my child back to me."

One day when Aigean returned from the lonely castle he found Duald walking by the sea.

"You remember, Duald," he said, "when I was a child I used to think I heard voices in the waves."

"Yes, you were always a child of the sea."

"Well, last night as I wandered here alone it seemed to me there was a sweet, sad song being wafted over the water?"

"From what direction?" asked Duald.

"Far away from the west and the faint sound seemed like the song 'The Sad Sea Maiden', the song Alainn sang the night of the ball."

"Oh, my boy, your fancy weaves a lot of strange dreams. Try to forget Alainn."

Aigean spoke angrily. "I never will," he said.

Though Duald seemed to pay so little attention to Aigean's words about the voice in the waves, he thought of them a great deal.

Next morning he cut a branch of yew and threw it far into the sea.

The wind was blowing from the west but against wind and foam the rod floated westward.

He went at once to find Aigean.

"Will you come with me for a sea trip?" he asked. "We will take provisions with us. The weather is beautiful and we can spend a few enjoyable days on the water."

"In what direction will we go ?" asked Aigean.

"Let us go westward in the track of the setting sun," Duald replied. Aigean always enjoyed Duald's company.

The pair set out and sailed over the water. All was beautiful as the golden sunset gave place to the pale light of the moon. "Listen, Duald, there is a song in the waves."

"It is far distant," said Duald, "but we will continue our journey westward."

All night long they sailed, each resting by turns.

At dawn they saw a rocky island jutting out of the water.

The song 'The Sad Sea Maiden' was now clearly heard.

"Let us land," said Aigean.

"The rocks are very steep" was Duald's reply.

As the light became stronger they saw a little cove where there were a few stunted trees. This was the only sheltered place on the island.

They made fast the boat. A large white bird seemed to hide among the trees.

The moment Aigean touched the land the bird uttered a low cry. Then, to his amazement, Duald saw Aigean kneeling before the long-lost Alainn.

"How has this come about ?" asked Duald.

"I can remember only," said Alainn, "that I went out in a boat with Finola. She took my pearl necklace from me. All the rest is a blank to me."

"Come home with us now," said Aigean.

"We will restore you to your father," said Duald, "and then tell you all that we know of what has happened since the day you went with Finola."

Twilight was coming on as they came near the witch's cave. The witch herself climbed up the cliff when she heard the sound of the approaching boat.

In her rage at seeing the occupants, she stumbled and fell and was dashed to pieces on the rocks below.

Diarmuid's joy was unbounded when he recovered his daughter.

"But," he said, "I have found her only to lose her again."

Aigean and she were married very soon after her return.

Duald was the most honoured guest at the wedding, and the pearl necklace the most precious among the costly jewels that adorned the bride.

The Wishing Chair

A Story of the Olden Time

"WE are a happy family," said Shane MacFadden, as he and his wife and daughter Roisin were having their supper one fine summer evening.

"Yes, indeed, Shane," said his wife, "but you have to work hard to keep us in such comfort."

"You know, Nora, I am well helped by you and Roisin."

"And, Father," said Roisin, "you also have managed to give me a good education and the opportunity to learn to play the harp."

Roisin gave much pleasure to her parents by playing for them in the long winter evenings.

They were indeed a happy family with no thought of the trouble that was to come to them.

Sickness broke out in the neighbourhood. The inmates of the little house did not escape. Both father and mother died. Roisin recovered. A sad and lonely girl she was.

Her aunt, who lived some distance away, said she would leave her own house and come with her two daughters to live with her.

"I will be a mother to you, Roisin," she said, "and Mella and Gobnait will be just the same as sisters."

It was a sad day for Roisin that the three women came to the house. All three were lazy and idle. They left all the work to Roisin.

The two girls were always arguing and quarrelling.

"I am tired of this life," Mella said one day. I

wish some handsome, rich man would come and marry me."

"You with your yellow face and long, lanky figure the wife of a rich, handsome man!" said Gobnait.

"Well, Gobnait, I would rather have my nice, slight figure than be a fat, heavy creature like you. It is well you have such huge feet for if they were small they would never support your big, bulky body. If you did not eat so much you might have a nice, slight figure like mine."

Roisin tried to make peace between them.

"You would both be much happier if you did not quarrel so much," she said.

"Oh, you need not talk, Roisin," said Mella. "Everyone loves you."

"Yes," added Gobnait, "and with your beauty you prevent anyone from looking at either of us."

"You were lucky, too, in having had such devoted parents and in getting a good education."

"Our parents took very little care with our upbringing," said Mella. "Even now my mother does not bother about us. She is either dozing at the fire or talking to the neighbours."

There was neither peace nor comfort in the house and Roisin was very unhappy.

One night the sisters were looking out the window while their mother was sitting at the fire. Roisin was trying to tidy the kitchen.

"There is the new moon," said Gobnait. "I see it clear in the sky and not through a tree. Perhaps it will bring me good luck."

"I don't care about the moon," was Mella's remark. "It never brought good luck to me."

"Oh, look!" exclaimed Gobnait as a woman passed by the window, "there is Ana Criona (wise Ana). I will call her in. She has always plenty of news."

The woman, as her name implied, was believed to be very wise. She had wonderful stories of the olden time. For miles round she was welcomed in the different houses, but she never stayed longer than a couple of days in each.

"Cead mile failte (a hundred thousand welcomes), Ana," said Roisin as she placed a chair near the fire.

"Though the day was warm the evening is chilly," said Ana, "and for an old woman like me the heat is pleasant."

"Well, Ana, what news have you to-night ? " asked Gobnait.

"Good news," Ana replied, "there is a new owner in Dunbawn Castle."

"That is the castle," said the mother, "where the rich widow lived. She pined away after the death of her beautiful daughter Maeve."

"Yes," said Ana. "The new owner is the widow's nephew. He is the last of the family and will inherit all the wealth."

"What is his name ? " asked Gobnait.

"Brian is his name. He is a fine, handsome young man."

"And who will live with him in the Castle ? " asked Mella.

"Oh! there are many attendants, but the principal one is Nuala, his old nurse. She has been with him since he was born. Both his parents have been dead for some years. I must be going now, for I have some distance to walk to the next house."

"Oh, Ana, don't go till you tell me my fortune," said Mella.

"And mine," said Gobnait and Roisin, speaking together.

"Now, girls, I cannot tell you your fortune, but I can tell you how to get good luck for yourselves.

I am doing this for your sake, Roisin."

The three girls gathered round her, anxiously waiting to hear what she would say.

" Your face is your fortune, asthore," she said to Roisin, " but it is your kind heart that will bring you the good luck."

Ana smiled as she said : —

" Now listen, girls.

" You all know the high bank at the back of the strand near the Black Rock."

" Yes," came in a chorus.

" If you climb the bank you will come to a field. Walk through the field to the stone fence at the end."

" Is it a long field ? " asked lazy Gobnait.

" Yes," and when you have crossed the fence you will come to another field, a larger one."

" Must we walk through that, too ? " asked Mella.

" Yes. And when you have crossed the fence at the far end you must walk through another field much larger than either of the others."

" Oh! I could never do that," said Gobnait.

" Well, if you could not, it is useless for me to tell you any more."

" O go on, Ana," said Mella. " Don't mind lazy Gobnait."

" Yes, go on," said Gobnait, "perhaps I could try the long walk."

Ana continued :

" At the end of the third field there is a little wood. The trees form a kind of circle. In the centre of the circle there is a stone chair. This is the Wishing Chair. Anyone who sits in it can wish three times. In this way they can get three things which they desire."

" I'll start off in the morning," said Gobnait.

" No," said Ana. " You must go in the order of

age. Mella first, then Gobnait and then Roisin. I must leave you now. I wish you all good luck. Good night."

"I'll get up at cock crow in the morning," said Mella.

"You will," laughed Gobnait, "if the cock begins to crow at midday. That is your usual time for rising."

"You are not such an early riser yourself," was the angry retort from Mella. Turning to Roisin, she said: "You call me when you yourself are getting up."

Next morning Mella left the house at an early hour. She walked briskly to the sea shore. When she reached the high banks she thought she would hardly be able to climb to the top of them. She made a great effort but by the time she had crossed the third field she was exhausted and parched with thirst.

With lagging steps, she came to the little wood. As she sat down in the chair she forgot everything but her desire for a drink. She cried aloud, "Oh, how I wish I had a drink of clear, cold water." Immediately the leaves on the trees overhead seemed to sing the words, "Your wish will be granted."

There at her feet she saw a well of sparkling water and a vessel at the brink.

She took a long drink and then remembered that one of her wishes was gone.

"My second wish is that I will have roses in my cheeks like the lovely colour that Roisin has in hers."

Again the leaves seemed to sing——
"Your wish will be granted."

All at once nice pink roses appeared in her cheeks, but there were thorns in each which pricked her.

The Wishing Chair

" Oh ! " she cried, " my third wish is that these thorny roses will go away. Bad as my yellow face was it did not hurt like this."

The voices in the leaves answered——

" Your wish will be granted."

The water in the well turned yellow and in it she saw her face reflected.

" You don't look very happy," said Gobnait as her sister reached home, weary and footsore.

" Never mind how I look," snapped Mella.

" Well," said Gobnait, " I will try my luck to-morrow and I hope I will come home happier than you are after your adventure."

Next morning, Gobnait rose early. She ate a good substantial breakfast, for she had always a great appetite.

Her experience was much the same as her sister's till she reached the wishing chair.

The fresh air made her very hungry.

" I'm starving," she cried out.

" I wish I had a good dinner."

The voices in the leaves called out——

" You wish will be granted."

There beside her, on a crystal tray, she saw a delicious meal. She ate heartily. Then she remembered that one of her wishes was gone.

" My second wish is that I will have a nice slight figure instead of being so fat and bulky."

The voices in the leaves said——

" Your wish will be granted."

Thereupon she felt her body shrinking and shrinking till her clothes hung so loosely round her that she looked like a long pole. Her feet seemed now to be enormous under her thin, lean body.

" Oh," she said, " I wish I had my own figure back again."

Again came the song in the leaves——

" Your wish will be granted."

All at once her own appearance returned.

She went home and ate a fine supper. Then she went to bed and tried to sleep off her disappointment.

On the third morning, Roisin got up very early. She left everything in order for the three lazy women who were still sleeping.

After a hasty meal she set out for The Wishing Chair.

The beauty of the morning made her glad. The sea was calm and sparkling under the golden rays of the sun. As she went through the fields she stopped for a moment to gather some of the wild scabious that grew on the borders of the fields. All was calm and peaceful in the brightness of the lovely summer day.

Still it was a very weary girl that reached The Wishing Chair. She sank down on the chair, worn out for want of food and rest.

Unconsciously she called out——

" I wish I could rest and slumber a while."

The voices in the leaves sang——

" Your wish will be granted."

Suddenly she was asleep and dreaming. In her dream she saw a tall, handsome man. He smiled at her and seemed about to speak. While still half-dreaming, she exclaimed——

" Oh! how I wish that such a man as that would be my husband."

The voices in the leaves sang——

" Your wish will be granted."

" My third wish is that I will soon have a home far away from my aunt and cousins."

The voices in the leaves answered——

" Your wish will be granted."

She began her return journey. After having walked about a mile she heard a cry from a small

tree by the wayside. As she stopped she saw a
bird hanging from one of the branches. A thread
or hair had evidently got entangled in its foot. She
climbed up the bank where the tree grew and set
the captive free.

The bird flew to a neighbouring tree. It
chirrupped gaily, as if to thank the friend who had
given it its liberty.

As Roisin was descending from the bank she
came upon a large stone and hurt her foot badly.
When she tried to walk she found she could not
move without severe pain.

Her home was far distant and very few people
came along the way. To add to her troubles her
dress had got badly torn.

Poor Roisin was in despair. She sat down by
the wayside and cried. After a while she heard
the sound of approaching footsteps. Round a bend
in the road a woman came into sight. To her
relief and delight she saw her friend Ana Criona
coming towards her.

" What is the matter with my cailin dilis ? " (my
dear girl) were Ana's first words.

While Roisin was telling her friend all that had
happened, a sound of wheels was heard. Round
the curve came a splendid carriage drawn by two
fine horses.

Ana rushed forward and stood in front of the
carriage. It stopped. The door was opened by
the footman. A young man alighted. Roisin
looked at his face and uttered a cry. She would
have fallen if Ana had not caught her as she
became unconscious.

The stranger was the man she had seen in her
dream.

Ana recognised him as Brian, the new owner
of Dunbawn Castle.

" Oh ! Sir," said Ana, " have pity on this poor

girl. She has hurt her foot and is not able to walk.

"Where is her home?" Brian asked.

"A good distance from here, if indeed it can be called a home for there will be small comfort when she goes there."

Roisin had now partly recovered consciousness.

"Will you come with her if I take her to my home?" asked Brian.

"Gladly will I go. I would do anything for the girl I love so well."

Turning to Roisin she said——

"Come now, my girl, good fortune has sent a carriage to bring you to a nicer place than the home you have left."

Still in a half-swoon, Roisin was helped into the carriage. Ana sat beside her and talked cheerfully, telling her all would be well.

The carriage stopped outside a splendid castle. When the door was opened an elderly woman with a kindly face came forward to meet Brian.

"I have brought visitors, Nuala," he said.

Roisin, half dazed with wondering, was led to the door.

"Well, my son," said Nuala, "if kindness and beauty are recommendations, the visitors have certainly a big share of both."

She led them to a fine room and placed Roisin on a comfortable couch.

Brian came into the room and soon Nuala had heard the whole history of the meeting.

"I must go to some friends I promised to see this evening," said Brian. "I will not be back for some days. Will you, Nuala, take care of our guests till I return?"

"That I will do and welcome," said Nuala. "Indeed it will be nice to have someone young in the house."

Soon Roisin was in a comfortable room with a dainty meal placed before her. Ana shared the meal and cheered the patient with the interesting things she had to tell her.

"Now, Roisin," said Nuala, "rest for a while. Ana and I will have a little chat."

When the two women were talking together, Nuala said——

"I have taken Roisin to my heart. Her beautiful fair hair and blue eyes remind me of my dear boy's cousin Maeve. I will be lonely when she leaves."

A far-away look came into Ana's eyes as she said, "Yes, when she leaves."

Gradually the sprained foot improved until Roisin was able to walk without trouble.

"Now, Ana," she said, "since I am able to walk again I should return home. I fear I have outstayed my welcome by remaining so long."

"Oh, alanna," said Nuala, "don't think of going till my dear boy comes back. He would never forgive me if I let you go without seeing him again. What do you say, Ana?"

Ana paused and looked very wise. Then she said, "My advice is that Roisin stays."

There was now the question of dress to be considered as Roisin's own had been so badly torn.

"Will the pair of you come with me to Maeve's room?" asked Nuala.

"There are many dresses there which the poor girl never wore."

Ana was lost in admiration of Roisin when she saw her arrayed in a magnificent dress.

"I always knew you were beautiful," she said, "but you now look like some wonderful creature from fairyland."

"Perhaps," said Nuala, "you would like to see the different rooms in the house."

" Oh, yes," was the answer from both.

" Here," said Nuala, " is the room where poor Maeve used to play the harp."

" Oh! may I play, please ? " asked Roisin.

" Of course, asthore, and welcome. Come, Ana, and I will show you the other rooms."

Roisin forgot everything in her delight in the music. She played on and on and did not notice that the door of the room had been opened until she heard a voice say, " Maeve." She turned round and saw Brian standing in the room.

" I fear I have startled you," he said. " For a moment I thought my cousin Maeve was back again. Please continue to play."

Roisin was unable to play. She felt as if she were again in The Wishing Chair dreaming of the handsome young man who now stood by her side.

Ana and Nuala came into the room. " Now," said Ana, " I can start on my travels again. The roving life suits me best."

" I wish you would stay, Ana," said Brian, " but I understand your longing to return to your old way of life, but I want to ask you to leave Roisin with us."

" Oh, yes, Ana," said Nuala, " please leave Roisin with us."

" Won't you stay, Roisin ? " asked Brian, " and stay always, for from the moment I first saw you I knew you were the girl I would like to make my wife."

" And perhaps later on," said Ana, with a knowing smile, " she will tell you of the first moment she saw you."

Nuala took Roisin in her arms, saying—" Oh, we will now have a happy home. My dear boy won't be lonely any more."

" But my aunt and cousins ! " said Roisin.

" Your aunt and cousins ! " exclaimed Ana. " If

ever they attempt to come near you I'll get all the bad fairies in the country to plague them day and night. Slan agaibh (good bye) now. My next visit will be for the happy wedding." With these words she hurried off.

The wedding was one of the grandest ever seen in the countryside and Brian and Roisin lived happy ever after.

A Prince In Disguise

PRINCE CORMAC was the only child of King Oriel and Queen Aoife.

The great desire of the parents' hearts was to see their son happily married. They determined to speak to him about choosing a wife.

"Cormac," said the King, "you must marry. Surely you will not allow the throne to descend to a stranger."

"And," added the Queen, "our great possessions to pass out of the family."

"But, Mother, I am content as I am. Where could I find a wife I would love as I love you? And where could I find one with such beautiful raven hair and sparkling eyes as yours?"

"You, yourself, Cormac, have inherited your mother's beautiful eyes and hair," said the King.

Cormac possessed many natural gifts. He was handsome and brave and had won the affection of his people by his kindness and charm.

Among his many manly qualities was his skill as an athlete. He was almost tired of receiving homage and praise for his achiveements on the sports field.

"Fergal," he said one day to his best friend, "it is because I am the Prince that such great tribute is paid to my athletic triumphs."

"Nonsense," said Fergal, "the applause is thoroughly deserved."

"Well, I intend to put the sincerity to the test. I want you to help me to disguise myself and I shall play as an ordinary hurler."

"And how will you arrange all that?"

"The players will be waiting for the arrival of the Prince and when he does not appear I in my disguise will offer to fill the vacant place so that the game may be played."

"Well, you have always enjoyed jokes and pranks. I hope this one will turn out to your satisfaction."

The day for the contest arrived. The players on both sides were ready for the game, but where was the Prince ?

"The match must proceed," said the captain on one side.

"Yes," agreed the other captain. "It would be unlucky to postpone it. It must be played to-day for the new moon will appear to-night and our matches are timed for the first appearance of the new moon."

At this point in the conversation Cormac, wearing a wig and cleverly disguised, came forward and spoke in a foreign language. Fergal answered him in the same language.

"The game may go on as usual," he said, " if this player is allowed to take the vacant place."

"By all means he will be allowed to play," said one of the captains.

"And indeed," said the captain on the other side, "we are all very thankful to him for enabling us to proceed with the game."

Opposite the ground where the match was to be played there was a beautiful castle. It had belonged to a chieftain named Niall who lived there with Maeve his wife and their daughter Etain.

Maeve had died and after some years Niall had married a widow named Sorcha who had a daughter, Grainne.

The second wife seemed at first to be very kind.

"I will be a mother to Etain, your dear child," she said, "and though Grainne is some years older than your daughter they will love each other like sisters."

There is a proverb in Irish which says "Time is a good story-teller". It had a sad story to tell about poor Etain. Her father died.

After his death Sorcha and Grainne showed themselves in their true colours. They were very cruel to Etain. Grainne hated her.

"Mother," she would say, "how is it that Etain looks more beautiful in her old clothes than I do in all my grandeur ? "

"Never mind, my dear. We will keep her out of the way and no one will ever know how beautiful she is."

Poor Etain had a very unhappy life.

Sorcha and Grainne were among the spectators at the great match. From a small hillock on the side of the field they watched the play.

Etain longed to see the game. She managed to steal out of the house and got a place among the crowd. Like all the onlookers her eyes were fixed in admiration on one of the players who outshone all the others. His movements were swift and accurate and it might be said that the game centred round him.

Suddenly a ball whizzed towards him. There was a wail from the crowd as it struck him. He fell to the ground just near the place where Etain stood.

In her excitement she rushed towards him and raised his head. As she did so the fair wig fell away and the black, curling hair was revealed.

"Prince Cormac, Prince Cormac," came the shout from the crowd.

For a moment Cormac opened his eyes and gazed at the fair face bending over him. Then he became unconscious.

"Let the Prince be brought to my house," said Sorcha, "and send at once for medical aid."

To the joy of all concerned the doctor said the

injury was not serious. Rest and quiet were all that were necessary for complete recovery.

Sorcha and Grainne were delighted to have the Prince for their guest.

" Dress in your finest clothes, my daughter, and sing your sweetest songs," said Sorcha. " Do your best to charm and entertain the Prince."

Now Cormac was particularly musical. The harsh, out-of-tune singing that he was forced to listen to nearly drove him mad. News of the accident had, of course, been sent to the palace.

The King was absent from home when the message arrived but the Queen set out at once to go to her son.

There was much delay on the journey. A rain storm had come on and travelling was very difficult. Shortly before the end of the journey the weather changed and the sun shone brightly.

As the carriages approached the castle, beautiful singing was heard from inside the orchard.

" Stop the carriages for a while," ordered the Queen.

The singing ceased but out from the orchard came a lovely girl. Her fair hair had come loose and had fallen on her shoulders like a golden fleece.

The Queen could not restrain her admiration.

" Fair maiden, what is your name ? " she asked.

" Etain is my name, your Majesty."

Just then a huge, tall man came running towards Etain.

" Hurry, hurry, asthore," he said. " Your step-mother is calling and you know the sort of temper she has."

When Queen Aoife reached the castle Sorcha and Grainne went down on their knees to welcome her.

" I am thankful," said the Queen, " for the

He was the best hurler in the game

hospitality and kindness you have shown to the Prince, my son."

"Oh, your Majesty, it has been a privilege and an honour to have him with us."

The Prince was delighted to see his mother.

After some time the Queen said:

"As we were passing the orchard I heard most beautiful singing."

"It must have been Grainne, my daughter, you Majesty heard," said Sorcha. "She has a wonderful voice."

"Yes, Mother," said Cormac with a slight wink, "she has indeed *quite* a wonderful voice."

"When we reached the entrance to the orchard a lovely girl came out. I thought perhaps she was the singer," said the Queen.

"Oh! Not at all," said Grainne, "she was merely one of the servants."

"Though she was poorly dressed," said the Queen, "she looked very beautiful with the sunshine gleaming on her golden hair."

"Mother," exclaimed Cormac, "I have seen a girl like that in my dreams."

"Your Majesty," said Sorcha, "the Prince has been delirious nearly all the time since the accident. Nothing soothes him but a drink which I prepare for him."

Cormac looked at the Queen and said, "Is it not strange, Mother, that I feel bright and strong till I take the drink. After having it I become dull and listless."

"The Queen turned to Sorcha, saying: "Thank you for your hospitality and kindness, which I hope to repay. I shall have arrangements made to take the Prince home as soon as possible."

The Queen departed but soon returned to take Cormac home.

Sorcha and Grainne were determined that

neither Cormac nor the Queen would see Etain. They had the girl locked in a room at the top of the house. No one was allowed to go near her.

There was only one person in the household who dared to befriend Etain. This was poor, simple Conn, who did most of the slavish work round the kitchens. He was a huge, strong fellow, but for all his size and strength he was very gentle and kind. All the animals round the house loved and trusted him.

Conn had a great affection for Etain. She told him all her troubles.

Very shortly before the departure of the Queen and Cormac, Conn rushed upstairs to the locked room.

" Are you there, my girl ? " he asked through the keyhole.

" Yes, Conn," came the reply.

Conn hurled his great body against the door. The lock broke and he was soon in the room.

" Come quietly, asthore. They are all getting ready for the journey. We will slip out by the back door."

Etain followed Conn. Before long they were out on the road.

The moon was shining brightly.

" Now," said Conn, " when we come to the orchard gate stand still. Leave the rest to me."

Queen Aoife, Cormac and their retinue left the castle to the great disappointment of Sorcha and her daughter.

When the carriages were approaching the orchard, Conn rushed in front of them waving his hands.

" Stop, stop," he said. " Look towards the orchard gate."

All eyes turned to where Etain stood in the

moonlight. Her beautiful hair stirred lightly in the faint breeze.

" Mother," exclaimed Cormac, " that is the face I have seen in my dreams."

Conn came to the carriage door.

" Oh, Queen," he said, " take pity on a poor, tortured girl and save her from the cruelty of a heartless pair."

" Mother," said Cormac, " please take the girl into the carriage."

" Oh," said Etain, " I cannot go without Conn, my best friend."

" There is room for all," said the Queen.

Etain remained silent after she had told why and how she had escaped from the castle.

No so Conn.

" Won't there be hunger and thirst in the castle to-night ? " he said, chuckling and rubbing his hands.

" You know, your Majesty," he continued, " Sorcha and her ugly daughter have fine appetites and like a good meal."

" And will they not have one to-night ? " asked Cormac.

Conn shook with laughter as he said:—

" Hardly, your Highness. I collected all the hungry cats I could find and shut them in the pantries. How will it be when the cooks go to look for the milk, cream, beef, fish and all the good things that the cruel pair will be expecting for their evening meal ? "

Not one of the company could refrain from joining in the hearty laughter.

The end of the story was that King Oriel and his Queen got their wish when their valiant son was married to beautiful Etain.

The Furze Witch

ONCE upon a time there lived in the western part of Ireland a king named Flan. His wife died when his daughter Lelia was very young.

Lelia grew up to be a beautiful girl. She was the pride of her father's heart, and his constant companion.

The great delight of both father and daughter was to ride through the country on their fine horses.

The king's favourite horse was named Duveen, from his black colour. Lelia named her horse Lunasa. It had been given to her on the first day of August (Lunasa).

One summer day Flan left home to visit a chieftain, who lived some miles away.

The lovely day was succeeded by a still more beautiful night.

The moon shone brightly and the air was soft and still.

" Gormlai," said Lelia to her old nurse, " I will take Lunasa and go for a ride in the moonlight."

" Do not go alone," said Gormlai.

" I want to go alone and enjoy the beauty of the country in the moonlight."

" I wish, asthore," said Gormlai, " you would take someone with you."

" Oh ! " laughed Lelia, " you are afraid I might meet *bean draoi an aitinn* (The Witch of the Furze).

" Did you ever see her, Gormlai ? "

" No, indeed, and from all I have heard of her I hope I never will. I believe her hut is underground in the furze field at the back of the furze hedge.'

" I know the furze hedge and the lovely little river that flows beside it. Some people say that the witch can be good as well as wicked. I heard that, if one speaks kindly to her, she might be helpful in time of trouble."

" Well, alanna, no matter what sort she is, I would advise you to keep out of her way."

Lunasa seemed to fly along the roads and through the fields. It was as if he wished to give all possible pleasure to the rider, whom he so much loved.

Lelia let him go as he willed. After some time he came to a running stream. There was a thick furze hedge all along the far side. Lelia knew she was near the witch's home.

She stopped the horse and dismounted.

From behind the hedge a strange, harsh voice called out : —

" I am in great pain. Come to my aid and rich will be your reward."

" I cannot cross the stream," said Lelia, " and, even if I could, the furze hedge is too thick and prickly for me to pass through."

The voice answered.

" Lead your horse along the stream in the direction in which it flows. You will come to stepping stones. At this place there is a gap in the hedge. Cross the stones and come to me."

Lelia led the horse along till she came to the stepping stones. She tied him to a tree and crossed over the stones. There lying on the ground she saw a strange looking old hag.

" This," she thought, " is the witch of the furze field."

" I fell and hurt my back," said the witch, " and cannot rise. Nothing will cure me but a drink from the stream."

"But where can I find a vessel to hold the water ? " asked Lelia.

"Look," said the witch, "by the side of the stream is a pitcher which I was about to fill."

Lelia gave the drink to the witch.

She was immediately cured.

"For your kind act," she said, "I will at any time use my magic power to help you."

"How can I find you again ? " asked Lelia.

"I cannot cross the stream," said the witch, "but, if you come in the night over the stepping stones, I will come to you."

The witch then gave Lelia a little horn.

"If you wish to see me again, blow three times on this horn. Here, too, is a magic key which will open any lock from the weakest to the strongest."

Having said these words the witch spread out her cloak and seemed to fly away.

Next day Lelia waited eagerly for her father's return. As the hours went by she became anxious.

Alas! not without cause. At night time two messengers arrived with the sad news that he would return no more.

He had always been a keen swimmer. Early in the morning he had gone into the sea alone. A man on the beach stood in amazement looking at his wonderful strokes.

Suddenly he seemed to struggle and in a little while he had disappeared.

"Oh, Gormlai," said Lelia, "what can have happened to my poor father ? "

"You know, achusla, his heart has not been strong for a long time. He should not have ventured into the sea alone."

Poor Lelia was broken-hearted.

"I have no one left to love me now," she said, "except you, Gormlai, and Art, your kind husband."

" Well, you know, asthore, no matter what happens we will love you to the end."

Lelia now knew she would have to leave the palace. The heir to the throne would come to rule in her father's place.

Cairbre, son of a haughty widow named Macha, was to be the new king.

By his request, Lelia was to remain in the palace till some time after the coronation. Cairbre was curious to see and know the daughter of the late king.

On the eve of the great day he went alone to the palace. Lelia happened to be walking in the garden as he approached the gates. He gazed in admiration at her lovely dark hair and sweet, sad face.

" How beautiful she is ! " he thought. " How splendidly she would reign as queen."

He turned away. Lelia had not seen him.

There were many handsome women present at the gorgeous spectacle of Cairbre's coronation. As he looked round he thought that Lelia was the fairest of them all.

" Mother," he said, when all the festivities were over, " I think I have to-day seen the girl who will be my queen."

" There were many lovely women at the assembly," the mother replied, " but in my opinion Lelia was the most beautiful of them all."

" Oh, Mother, I am delighted you think so. She is the one I will ask to be my wife."

Lelia was preparing to leave the palace. Art and Gormlai were to go with her to a house at some distance away. The house had belonged to her mother.

On the day before her intended departure, Cairbre came to the room where she was. She was looking out the window, thinking sadly of bygone days.

"Lelia," said Cairbre, "you will not leave the palace to-morrow."

"Why do you say that ?" asked Lelia.

"You will stay here and be my wife."

"Oh, no," was all the girl could say.

Cairbre looked at her in surprise and anger. "You do not wish to marry me ?"

Lelia rose from her seat and looked at him steadily.

"I do not wish to marry you," she said.

Cairbre went hastily from the room to find his mother.

If he was angry and indignant, his mother was more so. She was furious.

"Is the girl mad, refusing to be the wife of a king ?" she exclaimed, "and as well as that the greatest and noblest man in all the land."

"What will we do, Mother ?" Cairbre asked.

"What will we do ? We will compel the stupid girl to marry you. She is clever and beautiful and would be a great queen. I believe she is beloved by the people. I have always given you everything you desired and I will not fail you now. Let me think of some plan to bring the silly girl to her senses."

Later in the day Macha called her son to her.

"I have a plan," she said. "If Lelia still refuses to marry you, tell her you will give her three days to consider the matter. If at the end of that time she does not consent to be your wife you will have her imprisoned in one of the dungeons in the castle. There she will learn sense and gratitude."

When Lelia heard of the terrible fate that was destined for her, she went at once to her loved nurse.

" Gormlai," she said, " what am I to do to escape from this cruel pair ? "

" Wait, asthore, I have thought of a way for you to escape. Art and I will mount Duveen and you Lunasa. We will go like the wind and reach your mother's house before the cruel king will know we have gone."

In a very short time the horses were ready and the riders set off.

Unfortunately, Macha had been wakeful in the night. She heard the trampling of the horses and at once gave the alarm.

Cairbre called together a number of his attendants and started off in pursuit.

Lelia and her friends had not gone far when they heard the sound of the galloping horses.

Looking round they saw they were close behind them.

" Gormlai," said Lelia, " Cairbre will take me back with him."

" I fear he will, asthore."

" Will you, Gormlai, and Art take care of the two horses and continue your journey. The animals will be safe and well cared for by you."

Cairbre and his men had now reached the poor fugitives.

" Halt ! " said he in a voice of thunder.

Turning to his men, he said : —

" Use your swords if necessary. Take the girl and let the others follow their own course."

Art and Gormlai knew it would be futile to offer any resistance. They rode away.

In the midst of her trouble Lelia was consoled by the thought that the horses would be well cared for.

" Now," Lelia," said Cairbre when they reached the palace, " I have said I would give you three days in which to decide whether you will become my wife or be imprisoned in the dark dungeon."

"I prefer life in a dungeon to marriage with you," was Lelia's reply.

"Well, take two days to think over the matter," said Cairbre as he strode out of the room.

After a short time he returned and said: "Remember, it is useless for you to try to escape a second time. Every door will be shut and the keys will be removed from the locks."

These words reminded Lelia that the witch had given her a magic key. She determined to go to the furze field as soon as all the inmates of the castle were asleep.

When all was still, she unlocked one of the doors and hurried from the palace.

She crossed the stepping stones and blew three times on the little horn.

The dark form of the witch seemed to fly towards her.

When Lelia told her sad story, the witch said:—

"I can help you, but you must follow my instructions carefully. Wait here a moment." She disappeared but returned in a very short time.

"Take these," she said as she handed Lelia a pair of strange looking shoes. "You can wear them over your own shoes. They are made from bats' wings. You can walk in them without making the least noise. They will bring you over the ground as quickly as if you were flying. In a very short time you will be far from the palace."

"But where will I go?" asked Lelia.

"Take the road that leads westwards. Pass every house till you come to a beautiful castle. Go to the kitchen quarters and ask for food and a place to rest.

"You are sure to be received with kind hospitality. Next morning ask leave to stay in the castle as a worker in the kitchen. You must not wear your own fine clothes. Dress as a working girl."

" I can manage to do that," said Lelia. " Gormlai, my old nurse, has left some of her worn clothes in her room."

" One word more," said the witch. " On no account tell who you are. Let that be found out in its own time. Now hurry back. When all is quiet and still in the palace to-morrow night, steal out and away."

The witch vanished without waiting for a word of thanks.

Lelia put on the magic shoes.

In what seemed but a moment of time she reached the castle.

In Gormlai's room she found the clothes necessary for the disguise.

It was grief to her to part with her lovely dresses and jewels.

" One treasure I must take with me," she thought.

This was a *mionn oir* (golden diadem) which her father had given to her mother on their wedding day.

She fastened the ornament under her dress and hurried away. Such was the power of the magic shoes that she was a great distance from the palace before it was known that she was gone.

When the king heard she had escaped, he gave orders that followers should be sent in all directions.

He himself was foremost amongst them. In urging his horse to leap over a fast flowing river he was thrown and carried away in the rushing waters.

His death was such a shock to his mother she did not long survive him.

Lying on the ground she saw a strange-looking old woman

When Lelia reached the castle the magic shoes fell from her feet and disappeared completely.

She knocked at one of the lower doors. It was opened by a big, fat woman with a kindly face.

" May I rest here for the night ? " Lelia asked.

" Of course you can, alanna. Our good lady always tells us to have a *caoin failte* (kind welcome) for all who come our way."

Mor, as the woman was called, led Lelia into the big kitchen. She gave her a good meal and showed her a comfortable bed.

Lelia was careful to put the diadem under her pillow before settling to sleep. Next morning she fastened it securely under her dress.

When she went into the kitchen, Mor greeted her with a beaming smile.

" Your lovely face will be a delight to me," she said.

" But," said Lelia, " I want to be useful. Please tell me how I can help with the work."

" Well, go out to the garden at the side of the house and gather some fruit."

When Lelia went out, she noticed that the road led down to the sea. Just then she saw a small carriage approaching.

Suddenly, beside the place where she stood, a fox jumped over the hedge. It was followed by a great hound. The oncoming horse started and dashed along. Lelia noticed that the reins had fallen from the driver's hands. Her knowledge of horses came to her aid. She darted and, running for a second beside the carriage, managed to grasp the reins and stop the excited horse.

The driver was none other than Oscar, the son of Conor and Ita, who were the owners of the castle.

When he had quieted the horse, he turned to Lelia and said :—

"How can I thank you ? But for your prompt and brave action I, with my horse, would be deep in the sea."

Mor came out from the house. Lelia slipped quietly away.

"Mor, who is that girl ? " asked Oscar.

"I do not know. She came here last night and said she would work in the kitchen if I let her stay."

"Work in the kitchen with those delicate white hands ! " exclaimed Oscar. "Well, be kind to her, Mor. She saved my life."

Oscar was an only child and was much loved by both of his parents.

He had a very special affection for his mother and had no secrets from her. After his experience of the morning he sought her out to tell her of his adventure.

"I am sure, Mother," he said, "the girl is of noble birth."

"Well, Oscar," replied the mother, "don't think too much about her. You know your father is having a great ball. All the noble ladies from far and near are to be invited. He hopes you will choose a wife from among them."

A day or two before the time arranged for the ball, Ita and Oscar were sitting at an open window which overlooked a small wood.

After a time Lelia came into the wood and sat down under a tree. Thinking she was free from observation, she took out the diadem which she had fastened under her dress.

"Look, Mother," said Oscar as he started to his feet, "there is the girl who saved my life."

Ita looked more closely at Lelia. "Oscar ! " she exclaimed, "she is the image of the dearest friend I ever had ; the same beautiful dark eyes and hair. She was named Lelia. She died many years ago."

" Come with me at once, Mother, and speak to her."

When mother and son entered the garden, Lelia sprang to her feet. As she did so the diadem fell to the ground. She stooped hastily and lifted it up.

" What is your name, fair maiden ? " Ita asked.

Lelia hesitated. Then she said :—

" Lelia is my name."

" May I see the diadem ? " asked Ita.

Lelia handed it to her.

When Ita looked at it she said :—" I see here the names Flan and Lelia. Were these the names of your parents ? "

" Yes," was Lelia's answer.

" Then," said Ita, " you are the child of my dearest friend. I was present when she received this diadem from her young husband on her wedding day."

" Yes," said Lelia, " my father gave the diadem to me and told me it had been his wedding gift to my mother."

" Come with me, child," said Ita.

" I will have word sent to good old Mor that you are not returning to the kitchen." Turning to Oscar, she said : " When Lelia and I have heard and told everything, I will send for you."

" It seems a long time to wait, Mother," said Oscar as she and Lelia went away.

When Ita heard all Lelia had to tell about her childhood and later life, she was determined the girl should remain with her at the castle.

" Now, Lelia," she said with a kind, motherly smile, " your clothes are hardly those that should be worn by a princess. We are preparing for a great ball. You must have a beautiful dress. Rest a while till I return later on."

Ita then sent for her son to come to her.

" Oscar," she said, " it is your father's wish that

you will choose a wife from among the many beautiful and brilliant women who will be present at the ball."

" Mother," said Oscar, " I have already seen the girl whom I would like to make my wife."

The mother smiled, a knowing smile.

" My advice to you," she continued, " is that, immediately after the festivities have begun, you will enter the ballroom accompanied by the girl of your choice."

The ballroom was a scene of great splendour. The lights shone brightly " o'er fair women and brave men."

" But where is Oscar ? " whispered Conor to his wife.

" Wait and see," was her reply.

At that moment there was a murmur of admiration among the guests. Oscar had entered with Lelia on his arm.

Conor showed every sign of welcome and pleasure when he saw the girl Oscar had chosen.

Very soon there was a splendid wedding and, as the old story-tellers say : —

> " They had children in basketfuls
>   Rocked them in cradlefuls
>   And if they don't live happy
>   that you and I may."

The Spirit In
The Graveyard

TOM BRENNAN lived in a small farmhouse
in Co. Mayo. He and his wife and their two
boys were very happy in their little home.

"Brigid," said Tom to his wife as he came in
from the fields one evening, "I met Molly Moran
this morning and she said she was coming to see
you to-morrow."

"Indeed then she won't be a very welcome
guest," was his wife's reply. "She is the greatest
beggar in the country."

"I know that," said Tom, "but she was not
always as she is now. I knew her before you came
to live in this part of the country. She was a
bright, handsome girl and had a beautiful singing
voice. She was very intelligent and used to write
nice verses."

"And what was it that made such a change in
her?"

"People say that her brain was injured some
years ago when she fell near the quarry and hit
her head against a big stone."

"Well that may be, but she is a troublesome old
woman now. She neglects her 'poor man,' as she
calls him, and leaves him alone in the dirty little
house."

Next day Molly arrived. "I came, Brigid," she
said, "for the loan of a little money. My poor man
is very bad and I want to get him some
nourishment."

"Now, Molly, I know what nourishment you

will buy for your poor man, as you call him.
Indeed I will not lend you money, as I often did
before, as I know you would spend it foolishly.   I
am sorry to refuse a neighbour, but I won't lend
you any money."

" Well, then, Brigid, I hope that vou yourself will
want money some day and may you get the same
answer as you gave me."

" Here are my parting words :
   Now for your cruel scorning
   May your cows not milk in the morning.
   May your hens not lay
   An egg to-day
   These are my words of warning."

Raising her hand with a threatening gesture she
went out.

Just then the boys, Jim and Bill, came in from
school.

" Oh! Mother," said Jim, " you are very pale.
Are you sick ? "

" No, Jim, but run down to the potato field and
ask your father to come home."

Tom was not long in coming.

Brigid told him all Molly had said.

" And would you give heed to a crazy old woman
like that ? " he asked.

" Oh, Tom! Her words sounded like a curse. I
hope nothing will happen to the cows or hens."

Tom laughed. The boys laughed, too.

" I heard my grandmother saying," said Bill,
" that curses like chickens come home to roost."

" We must not wish," said the father, " that any
ill-luck should come to poor Molly. You know her
mind is gone and she does not always mean or
even understand what she says."

Tom went back to his work.

" Go, boys," said the mother, " and bring a
couple of cans of water from the well."

Now Molly did not go far from the house when she left it. She remained hidden behind some bushes. She saw Tom and the boys leaving the house and she knew Brigid would be busy preparing the evening meal.

Quickly and silently she went round to the hen house. The nests were soon empty. She placed the eggs in a bag which she always carried under her cloak and hurried away.

"It is nearly supper time," said Brigid when the boys returned from the well. "Go to the hen house and bring in the eggs."

When the boys returned empty-handed the mother was really alarmed.

"Oh," she said, "Molly's wishes have come true. What will we do if she stops the cows from giving the milk?"

Tom was puzzled when he heard there were no eggs in the nests.

"It is strange indeed," he said, "but I don't believe Molly's wishes prevented the hens from laying."

Just as supper was over a neighbour came in with the news that there had been a death in the village. Pat Breen, the shomaker, had died.

"I must go to that wake to-night," said Tom.

"No, Tom, Pat's wife is a cousin of mine and I would like to go if you will stay with the boys."

Brigid stayed a long time at the wake. There was much story-telling. One man had a thrilling tale about a ghost that used to be seen in the graveyard.

Brigid began to feel a bit uneasy as midnight was coming on.

"I had better be going," she said.

She hurried along the road.

Everything was bright under the light of the full moon.

Tom pulled the sheet off Molly

It was twelve o'clock when she reached the graveyard which was close to her own house.

To her horror she saw a white figure moving about among the tombstones.

She rushed home and fell into Tom's arms as he opened the door for her.

" Oh! there's a ghost in the graveyard," she said.

" Brigid, asthore, you must be raving," said Tom.

" Jim and Bill," he called, " get up and stay with your mother till I come back."

" Oh, Tom, you are not going to the graveyard," said Brigid.

Without heeding her words he hurried out.

When he reached the graveyard he stood still for a moment looking at the white object among the tombstones. Then he saw two or three cows near it. He went silently towards the figure. It was covered in a white sheet.

As he came nearer he saw that it was engaged in milking a cow while singing the following words to the air of the song ' The Pretty Girl Milking Her Cow '.

" You paid but small heed to my warning
But you won't know the why or the how
You will be without milk in the morning
Said the pretty girl milking her cow."

Tom pulled the sheet off the singer.

" Now, Molly," he said, " my pretty girl milking *my* cow. I have caught you."

" Oh! Tom, don't be too hard on me. I wanted a drop of milk for my poor man."

" Yes, Molly, and you wanted poor Brigid to believe you could put a spell on the cows. Tell me now, do you know anything about the disappearance of the eggs from the nest ? "

" Tom, my poor man wants nourishment you know and I took a few eggs to have them for his breakfast."

" Took a few eggs did you say ? Why, you know you emptied the nests. Well, come home with me now to your ' poor man ', but first I must go and tell Brigid all about the ghost in the churchyard."

After Tom had told everything to Brigid he went with Molly to her home.

When they arrived they found the priest there. Some neighbour had gone for him as Tim, the ' poor man ', was at the point of death.

He passed away shortly after his wife arrived.

She herself did not long outlive him. Notwithstanding all her faults, the neighbours looked after her in her last illness and laid her to rest beside her ' poor man '.

Fagan's Ghost

(Time: About the beginning of the present century)

A WIDOW, Mrs. Fagan, and her sister, Mary O'Brien, were the owners of a drapery shop in a provincial town.

They were keen business women and had amassed a good deal of money.

While seated at breakfast one morning they were discussing their plans for the future.

"I think, Mary," said the widow, "we have made enough money to enable us to live in comfort for the rest of our lives."

"Yes, Nora, we can now have an easy time. It will be pleasant to live in the country and have the view of the fields and mountains."

"The only thing," said Nora, "that I dislike about about the change is that Ellen seems to hate the idea of coming to live so far from the town. She was accustomed to plenty of company here. She said to me she wished we were going to the big house at the end of the street."

"I would not like her to be unhappy," Mary said. "Indeed, she has given us good and faithful service. You remember she was just seventeen when she came to us and she has been here for eight years."

"Yes, and for a long time after she came she did not wish to go out in the evenings. You, Mary, with your store of books made her very fond of reading and she stayed in nearly every night."

"Well," said Mary, "she is much changed in that respect. She goes out nearly every night now but, of course, I know the reason."

"Yes, I do too. It is since Barney Malone came to the place. I believe she is crazy about him."

"But they can't get married," said Mary, "for Barney is depending on what casual work he can get working in the gardens about the town and as well as that he has to help his sister, Maggie, who lives with him. I believe she earns a little money by working in some of the houses in the town. They are a good pair and it is sad to think they lost their parents while they were very young."

Just then Ellen came into the room.

"Well, Ellen," said Nora, "are you getting accustomed to the idea of coming to live in the country?"

"Well, indeed I am not, Ma'am, and if you will excuse me for saying it, I think the fine house at the end of this street would be far nicer and more comfortable than 'Woodlands.' That big, lonely house is miles away from every place. Some say it is haunted."

Nora laughed. "What sort of a ghost is seen there?" she asked.

"I don't know, Ma'am, but I was told there were terrible noises to be heard in the night."

"Well," said Nora, "if we hear the noises we will comeback to the big house which you say is so suitable. There is the postman, Ellen. Will you take the letters?"

"I hate these stories about ghosts and noises," said Mary.

"They are all nonsense, Mary, but it will be a long time before Ellen will feel at home in Woodlands."

After some time the two women were comfortably settled in their new home. Ellen was sad and in low spirits but she was faithful and earnest in her work.

One morning the sisters received a telegram. It

was from their brother who lived about thirty miles away.

"This telegram is from Maurice," said Nora. "It says he is seriously ill."

"Oh! we must go to him at once, Nora," said her sister.

"We cannot both go, Mary. Ellen would not stay alone in the house. I will go. I can catch the midday train. You won't be afraid of the noises if I leave you," she added laughingly.

"No, but I confess I would not like to hear them. I will be sleeping at the top of the house and Ellen's bedroom is on the ground floor so I will be far away from her."

"Oh, don't be foolish. I must go to see Maurice, though I believe it is only one of his imaginary attacks."

"I think so too," said Mary. "He is very careful of his health. If he sneezes he thinks he is going to get pneumonia, and if he has a slight temperature he thinks he has some kind of fever."

"I am not at all anxious," said Nora, "and if things are as we think, I will return to-morrow evening."

That night Mary went to bed early. She was awake for some time. At last she dozed off.

She was not long asleep till she was awakened by a loud noise outside her door. Then the noise passed down the stairs with an awful clatter.

Mary jumped out of bed and locked the door of her room. She did not dare to look out, but got back to bed and snuggled under the clothes, afraid to stir.

After a time the noise ceased, but she was still afraid to open the door. She spent some miserable hours till dawn appeared.

With the morning light she went down to the room where Ellen slept. Loud snoring greeted

Nora looked down from the landing

her as she knocked at the door. At last Ellen put her head outside.

" Ellen," said Mary, " did you hear the noises last night ? "

" Did I hear the noises, Miss ? Of course I did and I did not sleep for a long time. That is why I am so sleepy now."

" I hope my sister will come home to-day. I dare not spend another night like the one that has passed."

Nora returned in the evening.

" I found things as I expected," she said. " Maurice has an ordinary cold."

" Well, is he better ? "

" Yes. The doctor assured him there was very little wrong with him. Otherwise I could not have come back so soon."

" Oh! Nora, I am very glad you came back. I would not pass another night in this house if you had stayed away."

" Why, Mary, what has happened ? "

" I heard the most weird noises. They were terrible."

I locked my door for I was afraid to venture out even to call Ellen."

" And did Ellen hear the noises ? "

"Just call her. She will tell you all."

" Well, Ellen," said Nora, " I believe you heard noises in the house last night."

" Noises! Ma'am. A bad thunder storm would be nothing to them. Indeed, Ma'am, I wouldn't like to stay another night in this house."

" You must stay to-night, Ellen. It is late now and very dark and just as I was coming in the rain began.

Turning to her sister, Nora said :

" Now that I am at home, Mary, you won't be afraid. Let us have supper and then all three of us

will go to bed and try to forget the noises. I will
sleep in the spare bed in your room."

Mary was rather wakeful, but Nora slept soundly
till midnight.

"Nora, Nora," said Mary, as she shook her sister,
"the noises! Oh, listen!"

"Now, Mary, stay where you are."

Mary was glad to follow this suggestion.

Nora lighted a candle and went towards the
door.

"Oh, don't go out of the room, Nora," said Mary.

Nora paid no attention to these words. She
opened the door and went out on the landing.

Sliding down the stairs she saw a sweeping
brush, shovel, poker, tongs, bucket and other
household articles and near the foot of the stairs
was Ellen scurrying into her room and shutting
the door. Nora descended through all the
obstacles.

"Open the door, Ellen," she said.

"Oh, Ma'am, will you kill me?" said Ellen as
her scared face appeared at the door. "I could
think of no other way to get you to leave the
house."

"Come upstairs with me, Ellen," said Nora,
"and we will tell my sister the cause of the noises."

When Ellen was confronted by the two women,
she said:—

"Oh! Ma'am, oh Miss Mary, I thought you
might leave this house if you believed it was
haunted."

"And so you played the ghost," said Mary.

"You know it is very seldom I see Barney now.
I would do anything to get back to the town again.
We are very far from each other since I came
here."

The widow's thoughts went back over the years.
She remembered the time when a hard step-

mother had often prevented her from seeing someone who was as dear to her heart as Barney was
to Ellen's.

Mary was amazed to see the tears in her sister's
eyes.

"Come, Nora," she said, "let us go back to bed.
My advice to you, Ellen, is to try to rest after you
have removed these ghostly objects."

When the sisters reached the room, Mary said:

"I fear Ellen will never settle down in this
house. We would be very sorry to part with her.
She has been so good and faithful through all the
years."

"Listen, Mary, I have an idea. We will want
someone to keep and plant the garden. Barney
would be able to do all that would be required. He
could live in the cottage inside the gate. It is a
snug little house with four nice rooms."

"I know," said Mary with a laugh, "what's in
your match-making mind."

"Yes," said Nora, "Ellen and Barney will get
married."

"And who will keep house for us?" asked
Mary.

"I have thought of that, too. Maggie, Barney's
sister, could come in Ellen's place. Ellen could
train her into all the work. You know she herself
was not much older than Maggie when she first
came to us."

After a time there was a very nice little wedding.
Nora and Mary fitted out the bride in great style.

Barney and Ellen were a very happy pair. The
only time there was any sign of difference or
quarrelling between them was when Barney
referred to his wife as "Fagan's Ghost."

The Haunted Field

"NOW, Pat, don't stay out till after midnight," said Nancy O'Reilly to her husband as he was about to leave home.

"Never mind, Nancy. I'll take your advice and come home early."

"You say that every night but you are never back till the small hours. Then you are too tired to get up and attend to your work. You know, Pat, we are getting poorer every day."

"I know that, Nancy. If I was not so short of money I would never have sold the poor horse that had served me so faithfully.

"Well, it is never too late to mend and, I promise you, I will be home early to-night."

Poor Nancy had often got that promise before but never its fulfilment.

In the early days of her married life she had been very happy. Pat worked hard on the farm and as the children grew up they were able to help.

It was a sad day for the family when the father began to go to the nearby town to play cards at night.

At first he came home at a reasonable time. Gradually he began to stay out later, till at last it became his custom not to return home till one or two o'clock in the morning.

One day while Pat was still in bed after a very late night, Betty Cullen, the next door neighbour, came into the kitchen.

"Can you give me a sup of milk, Nancy?" she said. "My cow has gone dry."

Betty had a very loud voice. 'Betty the

Screecher ' was the nickname by which she was known.

She had usually some very startling news to tell.

" I was over in Larry Burke's house last night," she said. " They were talking about ghosts and Larry said there used to be a ghost in Mick Ryan's field beside the quarry. Did you ever hear that, Nancy ? "

" No, Betty, and if I did I would not believe it."

" Oh, well, I believe it. I don't know what sort of ghost it is, but they say it stamps its feet and rattles chains and, worst of all, it screams and roars."

Here Nancy had to frown at Annie and John, the two younger children. She knew they were ready to burst out laughing.

" Hurry off to school, children," she said.

When they went outside they laughed heartily.

" If the spirit's voice is any louder than Betty's own," said Annie, " the neighbours won't get much sleep."

" I don't believe these stories about spirits, Betty," said Nancy.

" Oh, well, I do and you should warn Pat to come home early."

Betty's loud voice had awakened Pat, who was sleeping in a room near the kitchen. He heard all her account of the ghost.

When she had gone, he came into the kitchen and said :

" Betty has always some foolish stories."

" You heard her ? " said Nancy.

" Yes, but I wouldn't mind anything she says."

" Well, Pat, take your breakfast and hurry down to the field or the potatoes will rot."

Pat worked hard that day but at nightfall he was off to the card house.

The horse was having a fine meal of cabbages

The hours passed and it was long after midnight when he started for home.

The night was very dark.

"I wish," he thought, "there was some other road home than the one by the quarry."

He passed the quarry but had not gone far when he heard the sound of rattling chains and tramping feet behind him. He hurried on through the darkness. The chains and tramping feet seemed to hurry, too.

He came to Betty Cullen's house. Betty had been wakeful in the night. As the noise came near, she opened her window. The night was so dark she could see nothing but she heard the sound of the chains and tramping feet.

Betty uttered three of her most resounding screeches.

This finished poor Pat. He staggered home and as Nancy opened the door he fell in a faint at her feet.

With the help of the children she got him to bed.

"Nancy," said he, "for your life don't open the door."

"Very well," Pat, "but I think you have let your nerves get out of bounds. Try to go to sleep and we will inquire about the ghost in the morning."

Nancy got up early next morning. Early as it was, there was a visitor at her door.

"You are welcome," she said as Mick Ryan came into the kitchen.

"Now, Nancy," said Mick, "will you tell me why did Pat steal back the horse he sold me?"

"What do you mean, Mick?"

"Come with me into the cabbage garden," said Mick.

When they reached the garden they saw a horse having a fine meal of cabbage.

A chain had got round one of its legs and made a noise as it moved.

" Oh ! " said Nancy, " that was the ghost Pat heard last night. The poor old horse was always very fond of him. That is why it followed him home. But I can't account for the screams."

Just then Betty Cullen came into the garden.

" Oh, Nancy," she said, " I heard the ghost last night. It was pitch dark so I could not see anything but I heard the tramping and the sound of chains. I screamed as it passed the house."

Mick pointed to the horse.

" There is your ghost, Betty," said he, " and you yourself supplied the screams."

By this time Pat had arrived on the scene.

As he came into the garden the horse uttered a gentle whinny and came towards him.

There were tears in Pat's eyes as he patted the faithful animal.

" Mick," he said, " I will give up the cards and work. Some day, maybe, I will have enough money to buy back my good old horse."

Ned Hogan's Ghost

TOWARDS the end of the last century there lived near the coast of Clare two families, the Hogans and the Kennedys. Their houses were separated from each other by a small field.

There was a long-standing feud between the fathers in each house, though the other members of the families remained friendly with each other.

One spring day, Ned Hogan came into his kitchen with a key in his hand. He went towards a cupboard in the wall. When he heard the sound of voices in the adjoining room he hastily put the key in his pocket and went out into the garden.

The voices were those of Mary, his only child, and Nellie Kennedy, the daughter of his enemy. Both girls were in the early twenties.

"I came, Mary," said Nellie, " to ask you to stay with us while your father will be away from home. Won't he have to leave for the fair in the very early hours of the morning ? "

" I suppose," said Mary, laughing, "you thought I would be afraid the ghost might appear."

" Seriously, Mary, isn't there a belief that a ghost follows your family ? "

" Oh ! that is said about us but I myself have never seen it."

" And you don't believe there is such a thing ? "

" No, I don't and I would not be a bit afraid to stay here alone."

" You were always courageous, Mary. So you will stay here without anyone in the house with you."

" No, my father would not be satisfied that I would, so I promised him that I'd go to my Aunt

Maggie in Kilmore and stay the night there."

"That means a drive of five miles, Mary. Why not come and stay with us when you would have only to cross the field ? "

"I know, Nellie, that you and your mother would have a welcome for me, but what about your father and Hugh ? "

"Now, Mary, you know perfectly well the love that Hugh has for you."

"Then he shows his love in a strange way. He avoids me on all possible occasions."

"It is pride that prevents him from showing his love for you."

"What do you mean, Nellie ? "

"Everyone knows that you are very well off and we are very poor. As well as that, there is a bitter hatred between your father and ours."

"Indeed there is, Nellie, and all on account of that bit of land between the two houses. But tell me, Nellie, what about your own love affair ? When are you and Jack O'Toole going to get married ? "

"Oh! our marriage will take place at Tib's Eve and that is neither before nor after Christmas. You see, I cannot leave home. Mother is so delicate and Jack would not like to come and live with all of us. I must be going now. Won't you call in to see Mother on your way to Kilmore ? "

"Yes, Nellie. I will walk with you now to the end of the field."

When Mary returned she found her father sitting at the table in the kitchen. He had a white wooden box before him and was counting the sovereigns it had held.

"Oh! Father," said Mary, "isn't it a pity that your heart is so much centred in the money.

"Did I not work hard to earn it ? "

"But what good is it now, hidden in a box

without use or profit ? It is only a cause of anxiety to you. Love of money is a terrible thing. It is like a hard ridge round the heart."

"Listen to me, Mary. I admit I have a great love of money, but I did not always love it as I do now."

"And, Father, what was the cause of the change in you ? "

"When I saw your young mother lying dead, I knew that want and poverty had been the cause of her death. I swore then that things like that would not be so for her daughter, and that I would win riches for you no matter what obstacles would be in my way."

"Indeed, Father, it is well I remember the long days when I was lonely and unhappy while you were working for the same gold over in New York."

"But I have the gold now—the fine yellow gold."

"Oh! it frightens me to hear you speak like that, Father ! "

"Didn't poverty take from me the creature I loved best on earth, your beautiful young mother. If I had had riches twenty odd years ago your mother would be alive to-day. Don't despise the gold, Mary. Not many girls will have such a dowry as you."

"That very dowry is the cause of sorrow and heartbreak to me. Only for it I would be Hugh Kennedy's wife."

"Hugh Kennedy ! The son of my bitterest enemy."

"Hugh and his father are not the same person. The father himself was your friend till you took the law suit against him and were given possession of the little field between the two houses."

"That bit of land was mine by right and was given to me in the Court."

" Oh, indeed it was and the case affected poor Tom so much that he lost interest in everything and pays hardly any attention to his farm. The little field itself is waste ground with nothing growing in it except the old alder tree near Kennedy's window."

" Why do you say that the money is a hindrance to a marriage between you and Hugh ? "

" Because the Kennedy's are poor and Hugh is too proud to ask me to marry him."

" Too proud! How does he know you have the money ? "

" Doesn't the world know it since the day Peg Clancy came in when you were counting the sovereigns ? "

Mary looked out through the window.

" Oh! Father," she said, " here is Peg herself."

" Well, if she is coming I'm going," said Ned, taking the box and hurrying off.

Peg Clancy was an elderly woman that was known far and wide as a meddling gossip. She revelled in being the bearer of bad news.

There was small welcome for her wherever she went. Mary was not at all pleased to see her but she concealed her feelings and receivd her civilly.

" God save all here," said Peg as she entered.

" God save you kindly," answered Mary.

" I thought, Mary," said Peg, " that you might be lonely here to-night when your father will be away and that you might like me to stay with you."

" Thank you, Peg, you are very kind, but I am going to stay the night with my Aunt Maggie."

" Very well, Mary, but before I go I would like to tell you something. I hope it won't frighten you."

Mary laughed as she said: " Nothing you could say, Peg, would frighten me."

" All right, Mary. Well, last night I had a strange

dream. I dreamt that your father was dead and his ghost came to visit me."

Mary laughed again.

"And what do you think that dream means ? " she asked.

"I am certain that it is a sign or a warning that there is trouble coming to you or to your father. The ghost always appears when there is sorrow in store for the Hogan family."

"Have sense, Peg. Here is my father."

When Ned Hogan heard Peg's story, he laughed at first and then said :

"Now, my good woman, this is one of your many lying stories. You no more dreamt that than I did."

"I tell you, as true as I'm standing here, I had that dream."

"Well, don't stand any longer but walk."

Peg went out in great anger.

"It is wonderful all the *pisreoga* she has," said Mary.

"Yes, but she never tells the truth and has always bad news. She is like a croaking raven."

As Mary was about to leave home, she warned her father to avoid Tom Kennedy if he saw him at the fair.

"Take no notice of poor Tom, Father," she said

"Never fear, Mary. I won't interfere with him if he does not interfere with me, but if he insults me he will get as much as he gives."

Tom Kennedy was out when Mary called to see his wife.

"Welcome, Mary," said Mrs. Kennedy, "the friendship between the women of the two houses is not broken no matter what the men may think."

"No, indeed," said Mary. "I do not forget what a kind friend you were to a lonely, motherless girl."

After talking for some time, Mary rose to depart.

Mary's father was counting the sovereigns

"I cannot stay longer," she said. "My cousin Bill will be waiting for me at the cross roads to take me to his mother's house."

Just then Hugh came in.

"It is a long time since we have had a talk, Hugh," said Mary.

"It is, Mary," was the reply.

"Hugh, Mary is going to meet her cousin at the cross roads," said his mother.

"I will walk that far with you, Mary," said Nellie, seeing that her brother did not offer to go.

When the girls had gone the mother said: "Hugh, you did not show any sign of welcome to Mary."

"What would be the use, Mother? I am no match for a rich girl like her."

Tom Kennedy left home very early next morning to go to the fair.

When he was leaving, his wife said:

"Now, Tom, be sure to avoid Ned Hogan. I know what you are when your temper is roused and Ned himself is no angel either."

"Never mind, Brigid, I'll try to remember the Irish proverb: 'Avoid the rogue, you need not fear the honest man.' Don't worry, Brigid. Ned will have his horse and car and I will have to walk home."

The next night there was great excitement in the Kennedy household. Neither Ned nor Tom had returned from the fair.

Mary Hogan came to the house hoping to get news of her father. Hugh had gone to the town earlier in the evening and had not yet returned.

"Nellie," said Mary, "wouldn't it be as well for your mother to go upstairs and rest a while?"

"Oh, alanna," said the poor mother, "how can I rest till I see the two men safely home?"

"Come, Mother," said Nellie, "and rest in the armchair."

Just as they were leaving the kitchen, Peg Clancy rushed in saying:

"Oh! I have terrible news. Wait until I am able to talk."

"Indeed, Peg, talk never fails you. What is your terrible news?" asked Mary.

"I was coming past the graveyard when I heard moaning and groaning. I looked over the wall and there in the moonlight, Mary, I saw your father's ghost. He was on his knees beside your mother's grave."

"My father's ghost! You are mad, Peg."

"Not a bit mad. Everyone in the town has the same story now."

"Oh! what story, Peg?" asked Nellie.

"Ned Hogan is dead and no one knows where your father is and, worst of all, the box of gold was stolen from your house, Mary, and everyone thinks Tom Kennedy stole it and ran off with it."

At this moment Hugh arrived and with him the priest, Father O'Gorman.

"You here, Peg?" said the priest. "Then, my friends, you have heard the worst."

"Oh! Father," said Mary. "I hope we are not to believe everything Peg has said."

"Will you please, Father, tell my mother all you know," said Hugh.

"It is with great sorrow, Hugh, that I give the bad news. It is said that Ned and Tom were heard exchanging angry words at the fair. Tom said something about the box of money as he was starting out to walk home along the cliff path, which is frequented by very few people.

"Ned followed him. Nothing has since been heard of either of the men.

"Oh! my friends, you do not know how hard it is for me to tell this sad news."

"We do know, Father," said Hugh, "but it is best that you should be the one to tell it."

Father O'Gorman continued :

"Tim Burke, the fisherman, was out in his boat this evening. When he landed he climbed up to the cliff path. He found a pipe on the sandy ground and saw footprints near it."

"Oh!" said Mary, "was it my father's pipe? He got one from a friend in America and it had his name engraved on it."

"I fear, Mary my girl, it was your father's pipe." Here the priest hesitated.

"Tell us the whole story, Father," said Hugh. "We must know it sooner or later."

"I fear you must, Hugh. Tim looked down on the cliff and saw blood stains on the side."

"Ned Hogan is dead," said Peg Clancy.

"Oh!" she screamed, "there is the ghost again," as a pale face appeared at the window.

Mrs. Kennedy fainted. While the two girls went to her aid, Peg ran quickly to the town to spread the news that the ghost had appeared again.

Father O'Gorman and Hugh hurried out to see the place from whence the ghost had come.

There in the moonlight on the damp ground they found Ned Hogan. He had fallen from the alder tree.

"Oh! Father," said he. "I am glad you are here." Then he became unconscious.

"The doctor is away," said Hugh, after he and the priest had carried poor Ned into the kitchen and laid him on the old settle bed. "The doctor could not do anything. Poor Ned is very near the end," said Father O'Gorman.

The weeping women stood by looking for some sign of life in the still form.

At last Ned opened his eyes.

Mary knelt beside him.

"I know," he said, "I have not long to live. I want to tell poor Mary everything.

"When the fair was over I found that the horse had gone lame.

"I left it with the car in the town and started to walk home. The shortest way was the cliff path. I overtook poor Tom and it was not long till we were arguing with each other."

"Oh!" said Brigid, "poor Tom was always a bit hot-tempered."

Ned continued his sad story. "In the heat of the argument Tom stumbled and fell down the cliff.

"Oh! that I had died before I saw him falling down, down till the hungry waves dragged him into the depths of the sea."

"You are not responsible for his death, Father," said Mary.

"No, but I am afraid I will be accused of murdering him."

"No, no!" exclaimed Hugh.

His words were echoed by his mother and Nellie.

Ned continued in faltering tones.

"I made up my mind to leave the country. I went to the churchyard to kneel for the last time beside my beloved wife's grave.

"Then I took the box of money from the house and scratched the words 'For Hugh and Mary' on the lid. I left it inside the back door here for I knew that door is on the latch till late at night."

With great difficulty poor Ned continued.

"While passing the window I heard your voice, Mary. I climbed up the alder tree to have a last look at you. The branch gave way and I fell.

"There in the place that was the cause of all our sorrow, I met the fate which I deserved."

The priest signed to Mary and the others to leave him and the dying man together.

After some time, Father O'Gorman called the waiting group to tell them poor Ned was almost gone.

Ten Years Later

There is happiness in the Kennedy household though poor Brigid is gone. She did not long survive her husband.

The place that was the cause of so much strife and sorrow is now a playground for happy children. Mary Kennedy looks out with joy to where her twin boys, Tom and Ned, play with their little sisters.

They are often joined by their cousins for Aunt Nellie lives in the adjoining house.

Some time after her mother's death she married handsome Jack O'Toole, who had long wanted to marry her.

Poor Ned Hogan's money has at last been of much service, for there are not in Ireland happier homes than those of the Kennedys and the O'Tooles.

Peg Clancy is some years dead. Though she saw so many ghosts in her time her own has not yet appeared to anyone.